THE DISTANCE

Dreams and Despair

JUDY POLLARD

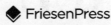

One Printers Way
Altona, MB R0G 0B0
Canada

www.friesenpress.com

Copyright © 2025 by Judy Pollard
First Edition — 2025

Yvonne Boyd, Illustrator
Trudy Norton, Illustrator

All rights reserved.

No part of this publication may be reproduced in any form, or by any means, electronic or mechanical, including photocopying, recording, or any information browsing, storage, or retrieval system, without permission in writing from FriesenPress.

ISBN
978-1-03-832798-7 (Hardcover)
978-1-03-832797-0 (Paperback)
978-1-03-832799-4 (eBook)

1. FICTION, WORLD LITERATURE / CANADA, 20TH CENTURY

Distributed to the trade by The Ingram Book Company

DEDICATION

This book is dedicated to my late husband Ted who intrigued me with tales of people and events in the Kootenay Lake area when I began spending summers in Argenta as a teenager. One of his favourite characters of the past was the notorious Red MacLeod.

Acknowledgements

~

*W*riting this book has been a long journey. After retiring as a college instructor, I enrolled in creative writing classes and was challenged to begin a new endeavour in my life. I'm grateful to Leesa Dean, my inspiring writing instructor, who gently led me in my creative efforts. Also, the support and feedback of fellow creative writing students was invaluable in my first attempts at creating this story. Most especially, I owe a debt of gratitude to Cari-Ann Gotta for all her assistance with content editing in the early stages of my writing.

My family members, particularly my daughter Deb and my son Kevin, listened and supported me through my explorations. They also assisted with sections of the book that required specific expertise, such as on the forest and mountain environments and the management of horses. Members of my writing group patiently listened to me, read pieces of the writing, and were kind with their feedback.

Many people assisted me with gathering essential historical and archival information to build the story. I am especially grateful to Greg Nesteroff, a local historian. A number of people shared with me family stories and photographs of life in the Kootenay Lake area in the early 1900s, and this information assisted me in creating detailed descriptions.

The Yaqan Nukiy display in the Creston Valley Museum and Archives provided an interesting variety of information about the history of the peoples inhabiting the areas around Kootenay Lake. This book includes interactions between inhabitants of Argenta and the Yaqan Nukiy, who travelled north on Kootenay Lake in their distinctive 'Kootenai canoe' especially during the seasons of fish runs in the lake.

While I was writing the book section about the trial, I attended an attempted murder trial in the Nelson Courthouse that continued for several days. The staff of the Sheriff's Service was extremely helpful in explaining procedures and all the details of such a trial. Others who were participating in the trial were equally helpful. Without their interest in my story and their willingness to share their experiences, I would not have been able to write the trial section with the detail that brings it to life.

I am excited to have original artwork included in my book. The cover is a vibrant painting of Mount Willet, at the north end of Kootenay Lake, by Yvonne Boyd. The portrayal of the Nelson Courthouse is an original watercolour painting by Trudy Norton. Thank you to my artist friends Yvonne and Trudy for sharing their talents.

Author's Note

~

This is a work of fiction that is based on a series of actual events. Through my research, I added interpretations of the implications of those events to describe the effects on the characters in the story. Most of the names of characters are fictionalized; however, there is one notable character who is authentic. Harry McArthur, my grandfather, was a schoolteacher in Nelson from 1918 through 1936, and he was the first principal of Trafalgar School. He proudly owned a Walton rowboat and, according to family legend, he rowed it north up Kootenay Lake to visit Argenta, and then returned to Nelson to attend the entire trial in the Nelson Courthouse. Unfortunately, I was not aware of the family story until after the death of my grandfather. How I would love to be able to hear his version in person!

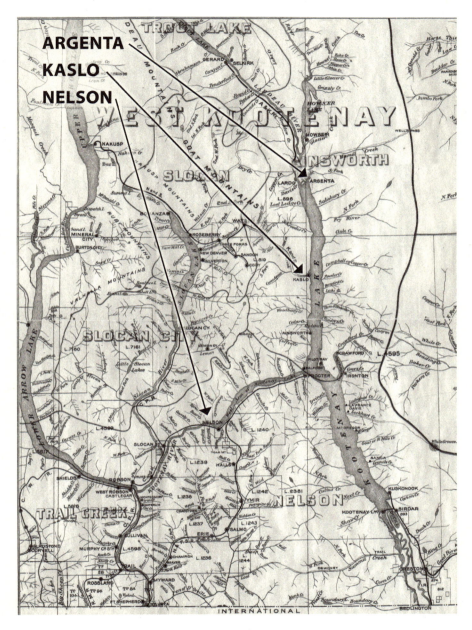

Map of West Kootenays
Drawn at Lands and Works Department
Victoria, BC
1909

PROLOGUE

~

The cerulean blue of the sky was breathtaking as the morning light intensified. First brilliant shards of sunlight speared between the double peaks of Mount Willet and laid the mountain's shadow over the precipitous cliffs on the far side of the wide lake. The guardian mountain possessed vision that extended into the distance. It accepted the truths of life and death without judgment, without accusation or blame. The early morning breeze down the mountainside was sweet with a light forest fragrance; it tickled the tall corn stalks in the garden, beginning the delicate dance that started a new day.

As was usual in the early morning, a tall, robust man prepared to milk his cow. His muscular biceps stretched the sleeves of his light shirt; his dark eyes reflected cool annoyance. Striding confidently toward the cow shed, he neared the door where a small man with a rifle was hidden. Without the tall man knowing, the rifle was carefully aimed at his chest.

Inside the shed, the small man was struggling to keep the rifle level as his heart galloped and his shoulders vibrated. The years of festering hate resonated through his body. He knew that if the tall man hadn't so carefully instructed him on the use of the rifle years ago, this moment wouldn't be happening.

JUDY POLLARD

As he pulled the trigger, rage burned in his throat, scorching the words, "You stole my honour!" The force of the rifle shot jolted his shoulder, and acrid smoke filled his nostrils, searing his tongue."

Late Summer 1932

~

So much easier than rowing my boat the entire distance to the north end of the lake . . . The steady pump of the steam pistons and the slap of the paddles make me sleepy. The lake surface is like glass—just as smooth as it was when I rowed all that way ten years ago. I should eat soon. I wonder what's on the menu for lunch. Hmm . . . who's that man over there by himself? Interesting—he's dressed in a wool jacket in this weather.

"Mind if I join you at your table? There aren't many seats left in the dining lounge," I said.

"Sure, I'd like some company. I've never taken this journey before. My name is Hans Johansen."

"I'm Harry McArthur. Thanks for sharing your table. I've enjoyed the trip on the *Moyie* several times; however, the conditions today are extraordinary and the scenery is spectacular! This will be my last chance to take this trip for a long time."

Hans responded, "Interesting—my first journey and your last journey." His blue eyes took in the vast landscape around us.

I nodded, peering closely at him through my smudged spectacles.

"Maybe you can tell me the points of interest along the way," he continued, reaching into his pocket and pulling out a stub of a pencil and a small scrap of paper to write down my suggestions. "I understand it takes about seven hours to reach Johnson's Landing."

Again, I nodded. "Yes, it's a long trip."

Hans sighed, a frown creasing his freckled forehead. "It'll be worth it to see my brother. That's where he is—Johnson's Landing."

I replied, "I'm going all the way to Argenta, the final stop after Johnson's Landing. Having a good lunch will help with the hours. The boiled fish and vegetable dish is one of my favourites."

Hans called the server to the table, and each of us ordered a meal of fish and coffee. While we waited for the food, we began to chat.

"What's your brother's name?" I asked.

"Algate Johansen. I've been told he lives like a hermit in his log cabin, so I'm not sure what kind of reception I'll get when I arrive. My cousins in Sweden think he might even be dead by now. They sent me on a search because I sold my property and had the money for the trip, and I speak English."

"I thought maybe you'd come from Europe recently. Your English is very good. It's a warm day. You've probably noticed that most of the men on the boat aren't wearing ties. I find it more comfortable to leave my jacket behind and roll up my shirtsleeves. Get some sun on my arms."

Hans agreed and immediately removed his jacket and tie. "Do you live in Argenta?"

"No, I live in Nelson. I'm a schoolteacher there, and I'm moving soon with my family to Kamloops. I have a new job as a school inspector. My wife and three sons are busy packing while I take a last trip on the Moyie."

Hans, with a quizzical look, commented, "That sounds interesting. It's a big job to move your family to a new place. I had to do that when

THE DISTANCE

my sons were in school. This trip must be important to you if you're leaving them to do the packing."

"Well, it's a very long story that leads me to taking this last trip to Argenta. Don't know if you feel like hearing it," I commented tentatively.

Hans smiled encouragingly. "If this boat trip takes about seven hours, that seems like enough time for a long story. And I'm interested. I would like to learn about the area."

I do want to tell the story to a complete stranger, just because I find it so compelling, and he seems genuinely curious.

"Here it is then. The story started many years ago, but I've only known about it since the trial ten years ago. In 1922, there was a trial in Nelson of a man from Argenta, who was accused of murdering his business partner. I attended all the proceedings. The complications of families' stories, the trial, and the outcome fascinated me. Before the trial started, I read about the circumstances and the charges in the newspaper, and I rowed my boat from Nelson to Argenta and back so that I could see where the murder happened. As you can imagine, it was a long and arduous expedition, and it took me about a week. The reason I'm making the journey now before I move away is that I want to see the family in Argenta. They have lived there for the last ten years, ever since the trial ended. I'm curious about them."

Hans looked up, his fork halfway to his mouth as if this brief beginning had piqued his interest. "Now I really want to hear about it. I'm all ears." I noticed the brightness in his eyes.

I watched his face while I finished chewing and then leaned forward to speak more softly. "I'm encouraged that you're so interested. Let's move to different chairs where we can observe the scenery along the lake." Hans enthusiastically nodded agreement and followed my lead to the lounge.

3

JUDY POLLARD

Fortunately, there were two vacant chairs so we settled in them and I continued. "I'm going to tell you the story in my way. My knowledge comes from my readings in the newspapers and my attendance at the trial, as well as a brief discussion with Wilbert after the trial. I am making educated guesses about the thoughts, feelings, and interactions of the characters."

1922

~

It was late summer 1922. Rumours were rampant about the murder at the north end of Kootenay Lake. The alleged murderer, Wilbert Jeanneret, who was an early settler from Switzerland, had been brought to Nelson to appear in court to face the charge of killing his business partner and brother-in-law, Thomas Rochat. When I heard about this, I couldn't resist rushing to the courthouse to find out what was happening.

A crowd had already gathered; people were pushing in front of each other to get into the courtroom and hear the charges read against Jeanneret. Squeezing past, I found a spot to stand just in time to hear the proceedings. The preliminary charge of the murder of Thomas Rochat was confirmed, and the trial date was set for the fall assizes in Supreme Court in Nelson.

People around me were talking about the men, and nobody seemed to know much about Rochat. However, one person from Kaslo spoke positively about Jeanneret, saying that he was an educated and thoughtful businessman who had personally contributed money to start a small community school in Argenta. Not the reputation one would expect of a person accused of murder. I was intrigued by the story. It was important to complete the trip while the weather was good and rowing to the

5

north end of the lake and back was going to be a challenge that I had not attempted before.

The shimmering expanse of Kootenay Lake reached into the distance as my Walton rowboat moved north. My perfect stroke was steady and controlled. The feeling of rowing this expertly designed craft gave me deep pleasure, and warm, calm weather made the long trip so much easier. Balfour was twenty miles to the east on the 'west arm' of the lake. I knew I could get halfway before stopping overnight. I was thinking about how interesting the conversations would be if I had somebody with me for the trip to talk about the mountains and the towns along the way. The geography was fascinating, and I knew all the creeks and mountains. As I rowed, the sweat ran down my face so that my spectacles annoyingly slid down my nose. It was damn annoying!

After leaving Balfour, I headed north toward Kaslo and found a campsite. Now the remainder of the thirty-five miles to the mudflats at the lake's north end seemed within reach. I felt the gentle breeze, fragrant with the pine scent of dense forests along the shore, and I soaked in the spectacular mountain views to the east and west. Seagulls swooped over my head, searching for snacks on the surface while squawking to each other. A fish splashed nearby, and I was glad I had my fishing rod so I could catch one for supper.

The steady rhythm of the oars allowed me to muse about what might have happened. The two men had been partners for thirteen years, and suddenly the relationship had erupted into tragedy. Apparently, both men were originally French speakers from Switzerland. I wondered if there could be some sort of family conflict that had started in Europe before they emigrated. As far as I knew, many Swiss people considered themselves to be pacifists. Could there have been animosity between them as a result of the Great War? It was even more mysterious that one of these men would kill the other. What had happened between them as they worked to create an orchard on the mountainside? There were many in town who believed the murder was a necessary act to protect a wife, which was a man's right, responsibility, and the basis of his reputation. I wasn't so sure about that and thought there were more complications to the story. Remembering the story that Wilbert took leadership in creating and funding a school for young children gave me a positive view of him as I too had worked toward the improvement of schools in my community of Nelson.

I was eager to get to the end of the lake and somehow find the spot where the shooting had occurred. I felt almost like an amateur detective searching for evidence. My plan was to hike around the area until I found the house, though I wasn't sure if anyone would be living there or if they would speak English. After that, I knew the row back to Nelson would be torturous, as my back and arms would be suffering from the first part of the trip.

There wasn't much time to do all this because the trial date was in the next week, and I planned to attend every minute. To complicate things, I had to be back at school in my new job as principal.

When I arrived at the wharf, there was no sign of people. At the small hotel nearby, I commented to the desk clerk on the lack of people around. He agreed, "It's quiet today. The *Moyie* doesn't come in till tomorrow then it gets busy." He seemed preoccupied, and when I asked where Jeannerats lived, he mumbled, "Up the mountain. They're not home."

Noticing many deer droppings in the thick vegetation, I walked slowly up the wagon road until I met a man coming out of a path. He was short and muscular, with purpose in his stride. Broad suspenders held up his woolen pants, and he carried an axe. He looked as if he was on his way to work.

"Hello," I said as I caught his gaze. "I'm new here. Can you tell me where Jeannerats live?"

He pushed his cap back on his tanned forehead and squinted from under bushy, dark eyebrows before carefully answering. "The house is pretty quiet right now. If you follow the wagon road to the next path and then turn up the hill, you should be able to see their place."

"Thank you," I replied. "I understand they aren't home, but I just wanted to have a look at the house."

"Ya, it looks just like a house in Switzerland," he grunted, as went on his way down the road.

After looking around and catching a view of the house and large garden, I decided to begin my return journey. So far, the weather on the lake was perfect for my row back to the south.

I became the quiet observer, discovering and compiling elements as the story unfolded, starting with their lives in Switzerland, where the two men first became friends and partners. Little did I realize the complexities that would soon be discovered in this tale of history and intertwining relationships.

BEGINNINGS IN SWITZERLAND

~

1908

Wilbert Jeanneret sat at his desk in Cook's Travel Agency. He felt comfortable being back in Geneva after spending three years in the London office. While he was there, he had been well trained as a travel adviser with expertise in both English and French. Customers often asked for him when they came in because his quiet manner allowed them to carefully explain their interests, and they knew he would be well informed and able to help them. Things were going so well for him, that at twenty-two years old, he'd been able to buy an expensive business suit with the raise he was given all because his language skills were in high demand.

His expensive wool tweed jacket was carefully tailored in such a way that it concealed the embarrassing rounded hump between his shoulders. He looked attractive as the subtle blues and greens in the fabric matched the sparkle of his twinkling deep blue eyes. The rosiness of his cheeks brought life to his kindly face. Although his hair was beginning to thin on top, he was careful to keep the thick fringe around the sides and back well-trimmed.

In his office, there was a supply of the *Cook's Traveller's Handbook*, a travel guide for trips in Europe and East Africa, which Wilbert offered to many of the clients. Because the handbook was written in English, it was important for Wilbert to provide a simple translation, as most people in the area were French-speaking and knew only a few English words. There were clearly labelled maps in the handbooks that made it easy for Wilbert to note place names and features in French so the client would be able to read the information at a later time.

Posters of British Columbia, Canada decorated the office, encouraging adventuresome people to migrate, purchase land, and become rich by creating fruit orchards. Colourful pictures showed lavish green slopes, apple trees in blossom, snow-peaked mountains, pristine blue lake waters, and beautiful young women lounging in the sun. Wilbert had often gazed at the posters, daydreaming about the "new world."

One day, a tall, familiar-looking young man, similar in age to Wilbert, happened to wander in the door. He wore the uniform of the Swiss Guard and had a dignified air. Effusing friendly self-confidence, he chatted with the young woman at the reception desk. Clearly smitten with his attention, she gazed at his handsome, lean face and muscular body. His dark eyes were a perfect match for the brown, wavy hair that was revealed when he politely removed his cap.

Wilbert watched the flirtatious encounter with envy and thought to himself that she had never bantered with him like that. To Wilbert's surprise, the newcomer strode over and introduced himself in French, saying his name was Thomas Rochat and he thought Wilbert looked familiar. "Do I know you? Where are you from?" he said in French.

Wilbert looked cautiously at Thomas and responded, "Neuchatel."

Nodding with understanding, Thomas replied, "We're both from Neuchatel. I think I was a grade ahead of you. I remember we played

THE DISTANCE

football on the same team. You had a great kick. And your brother was in my class."

Wilbert looked at Thomas with friendly recognition. "I remember you also. Didn't we travel to Geneva for a tournament?"

"We did!" Thomas exclaimed enthusiastically. "If I remember, we lost the first match."

Wilbert nodded agreement and then noticed Thomas's smart-looking blue uniform. "Are you in the Swiss Guard now?"

Thomas shrugged with relief as he explained, "Yes, and I'm finishing my term at the end of the month. Then I want to see the world." With a quizzical look, he asked, "What have you been doing?"

Wilbert stood up and drew himself to his full height. He could see that Thomas easily dominated him in stature and presence; however, he spoke with confidence, "I've worked for Cook's for five years, first here, then in London, and then they sent me back here to Geneva. I learned to speak English, so they wanted me in this office."

Thomas replied, "Can you read and write it as well?" Wilbert nodded somewhat humbly. "Well, that's better than me. I wish I could speak English," Thomas said with a touch of envy.

They stood side by side looking at the colourful posters of Canada, both wondering what to say next. Thomas glanced at Wilbert and commented, "I would like to go to Canada. Maybe this could be a way to get there. I hear they speak French there."

Wilbert nodded in agreement and said, "I could use some adventure before I get too old. French speaking is mostly in the eastern part, in Quebec, I think. Not so much French in the west where those mountains are."

Thomas groaned, "I'm dreaming about new horizons." He suddenly checked the time on the wall clock and said abruptly, "I have to leave, but I'll probably come next month when I'm out of the Guard to talk to you again."

After Thomas left, Wilbert began to muse about travelling across the Atlantic Ocean on a huge steamer. He had seen the steamers in London and passengers excitedly taking luggage on board. Now the posters and his conversation with Thomas made him dream more about it. He knew there were a lot of big mountains in Western Canada, so it might seem like Switzerland, and he could build a life there. But then he reminded himself that he had a good job already and money to spend.

The next week a large package arrived at the travel agency. Wilbert noticed it was from the Canadian government, and when he opened it, he discovered colourful promotional brochures urging Europeans to buy land pre-emptions. According to the brochures, it looked as if it would be simple to clear land and develop orchards, and then get rich from selling abundant quantities of fruit. His dreams began to swirl with lush, sunny mountainsides populated with apple trees and crates of fruit being shipped for sale. He liked the sense of freedom from European opinions and rules and just being able to do what he wanted, when he wanted.

Included in the package was an application form for land in British Columbia. Wilbert was excited. He read and reread all the documents. The application looked to him to be simple to complete since his present work involved assisting clients with applications for government documents, preparing for foreign travel, and often making all their travel arrangements.

When Thomas returned a few weeks later, now without his uniform, he seemed more casual and with a less superior attitude. Wilbert was delighted to see him and showed him the package from Canada.

12

THE DISTANCE

Thomas, impressed by the pictures in the brochures and the idea of making money, exclaimed, "Wow. I like the looks of it!"

"All the information is in English, so I'll translate," explained Wilbert. "These forms would be easy to complete. And I want to show you a letter from my friend at Cook's in the London office. He travelled to British Columbia. He mentions the great distance from the port of Montreal to British Columbia—close to twenty-five hundred miles. He also compares the landscape to the Swiss Alps surrounding Lake Lucerne and the rugged snowy peaks of Mount Rigi and Mount Pilatus."

"Really?" said Thomas, thrilled by the comparison. Lake Lucerne was his family's summer home and his favourite place. He chuckled as he remembered the cogwheel train ride. "Did you ever ride the cogwheel to the top of Mount Rigi?"

"Every summer when I was a child. I'll never forget it! The air was so clear we could see forever," Wilbert said with a grin.

Thomas's face lit with enthusiasm. "I think this is just what I'm looking for. What do you think?"

Wilbert, cautious as usual, nodded. "I've been thinking a lot. My family would say I'm crazy to give up my good job. Can we talk about it some more?"

Smiling, Thomas met Wilbert's gaze and agreed. "Let's have dinner. We can talk more. I'm glad you can read and write in English to help me understand the papers."

The two men enjoyed each other's company over dinner and shared dreams of travelling on a steamship to North America. The idea of escaping the stuffiness of the old ways and learning a pioneering life was thrilling. Several glasses of frothy beer spurred their imaginations, and they laughed together about the wealth that could bulge their pockets.

"Of course it will cost us to travel. I have some savings," said Wilbert.

"I didn't get paid much in the Guard, but I have an inheritance," commented Thomas. "I just want to get away from all the old-fashioned rules here. I've had years of rules after rules."

Wilbert vigorously nodded in agreement. "I'll write for more information about pre-emptions, and I'll find out how quickly applications can be processed. In the meantime, I can begin completing the application forms. And I'll start sharing my ideas with my sisters and brother."

Thomas said, "I'll go home to visit my family. I want to celebrate finishing my term with the Swiss Guard and talk with them about making a big change in my life. I know they'll want to support me."

Wilbert responded, "I'll contact you as soon as I have a response from Canada, and then we can meet again."

Within a month, the letter came to Wilbert from Canada with strong encouragement to return the application form quickly so that it could be processed by the spring. If this could be achieved, they could go to British Columbia by next summer, which was a more hospitable time of the year for long-distance travel in Canada and a much easier time to set up a living situation in a remote mountainous area.

The two young men moved forward with plans. Their families gave their blessings. However, apprehensions began to push into Wilbert's consciousness: *Can I do the physical work? Can I live closely with Thomas?* He knew life would be very different from his present secure job sitting behind a desk and helping customers. There would be many risks and no regular salary.

One of Wilbert's older brothers, Hubert, heard about the plan and became insistent that he should go along. Hubert and Wilbert were ten years apart. Wilbert tended to be more silent, keeping his thoughts to himself and quietly studying his own interests. His proficiency for languages had been evident in school, and he was encouraged to take work in different situations where his language abilities were much appreciated.

Hubert was similar in height to Wilbert; however, he was more muscular and highly energetic. He had been a star soccer player and proudly acknowledged any recognition of his athletic skills. His reputation as a hard worker had ensured his employment in different work situations, and most recently, he had been employed by the French government in airplane construction.

Neither Wilbert nor Hubert had been fortunate when searching for a wife, perhaps because they didn't know how to find one. Both men were shy around women, even though they had four sisters. The family was religious and attended church every weekend. Living in a small community meant everybody knew each other and gossip thrived, especially gossip about infidelities in marriages. Wilbert had no patience for such talk as he found the idea disgusting.

After a family dinner, Hubert said, "Wilbert I've been thinking. How about I come too? I've had steady work and have some savings. It would be useful to have me along if the work is as demanding as you've been told."

Wilbert looked curiously at his brother, wondering if he really meant what he was saying. Hubert's dark gaze seemed serious. "Let me think about it. What makes you think you want to come?"

"I just want a change in my life. If I stay here and a war starts, I'll be the one responsible for protecting everybody."

Wilbert nodded showing his understanding. "I'll talk with Thomas. I like the idea. You and I get along pretty well. You might need to get some more dress-up clothes for the trip on the ocean liner. I think they have formal dinners."

As Hubert argued his case, Wilbert began to think about the advantages of bringing his brother along, especially since he had always felt like a weakling and was self-conscious about the rounded back that had burdened him since childhood. The teasing and bullying he suffered were a thundercloud in his memory. Hubert had often been Wilbert's protector. Although Hubert and Wilbert were a decade apart, they had been close as children. However, they had grown apart in recent years as adult responsibilities kept them busy in different parts of the world.

So Wilbert approached Thomas about including Hubert. After some debate, Thomas agreed, although he had known Hubert when they played football on opposite teams and secretly thought he was something of a bully. Thomas did have concerns about whether Wilbert was up to the demands of the physical work, so he realized it might be advantageous to include Hubert. And with three of them, it would be possible to make more money from their work.

Once the application was approved, the next challenge was securing passage on a steamer—a task Wilbert took on. Through Cook's Travel, he managed to have his own ticket supplied as a termination payment, along with a half-price ticket for his brother. Because Wilbert had handled most of the arrangements so far and was unsure of Thomas's reliability, he decided to keep the special deals on the tickets to himself. Wilbert reasoned that this was the best way to be sure Thomas would follow through with paying for his share for the trip and the land.

Although Thomas had assured him that he would come up with the money, Wilbert had heard gossip from his relatives—stories about Thomas gambling away his inheritance and frequently borrowing money. In the end, Thomas received money from his parents to cover the cost of his ticket and a deposit on the land. When Wilbert learned about the loan, it only reinforced his apprehension about Thomas's financial dependability.

THE TRIP TO THE KOOTENAYS

~

Spring 1909

The weeks of preparation sped by, and in April of 1909, all three men boarded the ocean liner. The ship was more glamorous than they expected with an ornate dining room, brilliant chandeliers, and tables set with snow-white linen cloths and silver cutlery. To Wilbert, it was like a fantasy scene from a novel complete with waiters dressed in black slacks, crisp white dress shirts, and vests, set off with black bow ties. These servers roamed through the dining hall offering trays of fragrant delicacies while the musicians impressed with popular dance melodies.

Many of the men had wives and sisters with them, so there was lively chatter and laughter. Beer flowed freely, and spirits were lively. Clouds of cigarette, cigar, and pipe smoke hung over many of the tables.

Three eligible young men travelling together were interesting and attracted the attention of other passengers. Thomas exuded charm, easily persuading women to sit with him at the table. He was a skilled dancer, and both Wilbert and Hubert watched with admiration as he gracefully guided partners around the dance floor. Wilbert recognized "The Garden of Dreams," a popular waltz that he liked. As the music stopped, Thomas turned to the table where Wilbert was sitting and gently and skillfully steered the young woman towards the seat beside Wilbert. She was wearing an elegant blue satin gown with a revealing neckline that effectively enhanced her creamy white chest. Thomas winked and said, "Wilbert, I'd like you to meet Maria."

Wilbert realized Thomas's intention and felt panic rising inside. A flock of excited birds was swirling in his brain. The chair beside him seemed too close, so he clumsily nudged his chair farther away as she sat down. "*Comment alléz-vous?*"

Maria smiled as she demurely looked sideways at Wilbert. "I'm well, thank you. You must be Thomas's friend from Switzerland. What town are you from?"

Wilbert could not resist the warm depth of her dark brown eyes. The subtle scent of lily-of-the-valley perfume was evident as Maria leaned toward him, filling the space between them, and stirring something in him as she leaned closer. He could feel the heat rising in his neck and knew that soon he would be blushing. Wilbert looked away and muttered softly, "Neuchatel and Geneva." Clearing the lump in his throat, he managed, "Where are you from?"

Maria, seeming uncomfortable with Wilbert's obvious shyness, tried to continue the conversation, "Geneva! What part of town did you live in?"

"Um, the business centre." Wilbert desperately wished he could think of something to say about travelling, his favourite subject. He looked around the room to get an idea and noticed that his fingers felt like icicles.

Just then, Maria looked up as another man approached and asked her to dance. Relieved to escape the awkward conversation, she jumped out of her chair, took his arm, and skipped off to the dance floor. "Nice to meet you, Wilbert."

Wilbert heaved a sigh of relief. At that moment, Thomas noticed Maria leaving and leaned over Wilbert with a sardonic smirk. "You'll never be able to find a wife if you can't even flirt a bit!" Although annoyed at the comment, Wilbert agreed that Thomas was probably right, and he would be committed to a life imprisoned in his loneliness.

Some evenings Hubert stayed in the dance hall with Thomas, increasingly enjoying the company of the women whom Thomas introduced him to, and even began to try dancing. Wilbert felt embarrassed. He didn't know what to say or do, so he went to the cabin by himself.

The ship docked in Montreal with much fanfare. The dock was crowded with carts, wagons, and carriages. Horses, nervous because of the commotion, neighed and restlessly pawed their hooves on the cobblestones. Drivers called out, trying to attract passengers. Although the three travellers had understood that Montreal was French-speaking, they were surprised when the language was so different from their Swiss French. Wilbert's ability to speak both French and English helped with the clumsy communication.

Horse-drawn carriages taxied passengers and luggage to the train station, and soon the next leg of the journey began—a two-week trip across part of Canada. The first train they boarded had three passenger cars and a dining car—much more luxurious than they expected. The benches of the seats in the passenger car were wide enough to sleep on, with high backs, and cushioning solidly packed with horse-hair. Wide windows provided excellent views of the passing countryside. The prairies with endless miles of grasslands amazed them. They enjoyed the view as they partook of the well-prepared food in the dining car. When the train reached Medicine Hat, Alberta, the threesome stopped for the night in a hotel, and the next day boarded a train with only one passenger car and no dining car. The porter had advised them to purchase food before changing trains, so they had a basket of enough food to last the final two days of travel to Nelson.

By the time the men arrived in Nelson, they were exhausted. The last portion to endure was a slow sternwheeler trip to the north end of Kootenay Lake. They sat in the lounge listening to the regular slap of the paddles on the water as the vessel was propelled forward. The mountains really did remind them of home in Switzerland, especially of Lake Lucerne. Majestic, sharp peaks were still smothered in pure white. There were long sweeps of avalanche paths that began in the high snows and led into the depths of creek draws below. Heavily wooded steep slopes blended into narrow beaches along the lake's edge.

When the sternwheeler arrived at the dock in Argenta, they retrieved their belongings and stood looking at the wide sweep of forested mountainside before them with some dismay. There were several small, cleared areas, but thousands of trees stood in the way of the orchards they had envisioned creating.

Hubert was concerned and puzzled. "What do we do now? Thomas, I thought you said there was a place to stay. All I can see is a mountain full of trees. The air smells sweet though." The air was remarkably clear and pungent with rich scents of cedar and fir trees.

"*Oui*, too many trees! The deckhand who spoke French told me there is a small hotel on the hillside here," Thomas replied, looking around with a worried frown. "Oh, I can see it at the top of the ramp to the deck just on the right. Let's go." Wilbert and Hubert picked up their luggage and tried to catch up with Thomas.

"We're each getting a room," Wilbert blurted emphatically. "I want some space to myself. We've been in close quarters for a long time."

Thomas, charging up the hill ahead of them, called over his shoulder, "One of you has to share with me because I'm out of money until I get more from my family."

Wilbert burst out, "*Mon Dieu!*" and stopped dead in his tracks.

With a look of annoyance, Hubert grumbled, "We all agreed to pay our own way! You said you had enough money."

The entrance to the hotel stood open in front of them. Although they were on the verge of entering, they stood confronting each other. Wilbert and Hubert glared and fumed. Thomas, slightly chagrined, said plaintively, "Don't worry, I'll pay you back. They said they would send money as soon as I tell them where to send it."

With further pleading and reassurance from Thomas that he would give them a promissory note when he knew the cost of the room, the three agreed that Wilbert should negotiate with the hotel clerk in English. They now knew that few people in British Columbia spoke French. Wilbert's talents were becoming very useful.

The three men stayed in the hotel, all reluctantly sharing one small room, while they sorted out their next plans. Maps of the site of the land pre-emption had been provided. It was a huge swath of 120 acres, high on the side of Mount Willet. The area needed to be explored, and they didn't really know how to start.

In the meantime, Thomas, who had been practising and was now able to speak a few words in English, found out who else lived in the area and managed to make a deal with a rancher, Mr. Hanna, who lived on the flats at the head of the lake. Hanna's wife was able to speak a few words in French, so she helped with the communication. Thomas explained that Hanna had offered to take them up the creek draw to find the coordinates for the land.

"He seems to know a lot about how to take measurements on the land," Thomas said confidently. "If we look at the map here, I'll show you where he says we need to go. He'll meet us at the trail across from the hotel in two days."

They studied the map before hiking up the trail until they came to a flat bench of land. Afraid of getting lost if they continued, they decided to return to the hotel and wait for Hanna to guide them through the thick forest to find the creek gulley.

Hanna was a tall, weathered-looking man with a confident, energetic stride. He was easy to talk with. The gaze of his grey eyes was direct and attentive. Wilbert was reassured that they would be safe with Hanna's assistance.

In preparation for the hike with Hanna, Wilbert showed them the supplies he had collected for the packs. "We can get water from the creek."

"What about animals? Maybe we need a gun?" questioned Hubert with temerity. "The wild animals here will be different than what we have at home."

"Well, Hanna says there are lots of bears, sometimes cougars, but they're sneaky. I'm glad there are three of us," said Thomas boldly. "And then there are the mosquitoes! They drive me crazy. A rifle won't do any good for that. But we need to find a gun. Wilbert, can you pay for a rifle? I can search around for one to buy if you can pay."

Wilbert, with a smirk of satisfaction, pulled something out from under the bed. "Look what I got! The man down the hall is going back to the States, and he sold me his rifle. He said he's only used it half a dozen times." Wilbert could hardly contain his delight at having one up on Thomas. He winked at Hubert. Finally, there was some sparkle back in his eyes after the exhaustion of the long trip.

Astonished, Thomas blurted, "Let me see! I can't believe you bought a rifle. You've never handled a gun in your life. I'll give you shooting lessons when we get out there. I know about this kind of gun."

"Good for you, Wilbert. Quick thinking. Need to have the gun before we can have lessons!" Hubert growled, looking directly at Thomas.

"I even got a good deal on it," replied Wilbert, as he and Hubert went out the door and down the hall together. "Let's go get some lunch, Hubert."

A few days later Hanna led them up the mountain, showing them the boundaries of the property and the location of the creek. All three men agreed that his assistance was invaluable. They found the thick woods full of mosquitoes that were a threat to their sanity. A rifle didn't help with that problem, but it made them feel safer when it came to bears.

For weeks they trudged up the mountainside searching for the boundaries of their land. Wilbert noticed the quietness in the woods. "The only animals I notice are the squirrels and birds, and sometimes a white-tailed deer. Haven't heard or seen bears yet."

"We'd hear them crashing through the brush if we disturbed them. I know they're out there," was Thomas's response.

Hanna had a lot of advice about how to establish the boundaries of their pre-emption and how to proceed with clearing the land—work they hadn't done in Europe. Eventually they were able to rent a cabin near Hanna's house and in turn did some logging work for him to earn cash. Hanna, an astute businessman, was well acquainted with the many miners and farmers who were arriving in the area, and he knew how to benefit from relationships with them.

*

"It's daunting to realize all that these Swiss immigrants needed to learn about," I commented to Hans.

Hans shook his head. "I don't see how they managed to learn about it and do the physical work."

"Exhaustion and stubbornness, no doubt," I replied. "They were fortunate to have people to assist them. I wonder if they realized how important that was. There was probably lots of tension building between them."

WORKING THE LAND

~

Spring 1911-Early 1914

Two years after their arrival in Argenta, Thomas invested in a boat with an unreliable motor. He worked for Hanna on Duncan River, retrieving logs and towing them to the log boom at the edge of the lake near the flats. Wilbert and Hubert, although they weren't comfortable working in a boat on the river, sometimes joined Thomas to make some extra cash.

It was a soft, fragrant day in early June. The stands of cottonwood trees edging the banks of the river channel were thickly burdened with bright green spring leaves. The oxygen-rich air was invigorating. Thomas wanted to get some work done on the river, but Wilbert and Hubert were hesitant. With his usual confident style, Thomas said, "Come on. I promised Hanna I would find more of the logs and break up the log jams today."

"I don't like this," grumbled Wilbert. "That river's running high, and I'm not so sure about your motor."

"*Oui*, it breaks down every day," agreed Hubert. "I don't want to get dumped. And I don't swim. Never did like it. And I'm not good with a pike pole. I don't want to go."

Thomas's tone of voice became more emphatic as he realized they might refuse to go, and he needed the help. "Don't worry, it's okay. Get in the boat. I fixed the motor."

"All right," muttered Wilbert, "at least the mosquitoes aren't after us when we're on the river."

Thomas directed the boat into the mouth of the river channel, which narrowed soon after they moved upstream. Spring runoff was at its peak, with water pushing high above banks and frothing into the roots of giant cottonwood trees. Eddies swirled round and round, often backwards in the current. As Thomas manoeuvred the boat into the deep corners, they caught the scent of rotten, decaying mounds of leaves and debris that were amassed along the banks.

As they had feared, the boat was pushed erratically by the currents even with Thomas's strong hand at the tiller. With a view from the centre of the boat, Wilbert and Hubert watched, hearts in their mouths. Compared to the smooth gurgling at the river's mouth, the water there began to sound angry. A deep vortex swirled before their eyes as it sucked the water deep into the stream below the boat. Hubert poked Wilbert's arm. "I don't like this," he mumbled. Wilbert vehemently nodded agreement and turned to Thomas to get his attention.

"We should turn around, Thomas. This is too dangerous!"

Thomas shook his head and steered the boat into a more calm position. "It's no problem. There are some logs at this corner. I'll get closer, and you can reach them."

Hubert and Wilbert's job was to catch logs using a ten-foot-long wooden pike pole with a sharp metal hook attached to the end. Reaching as far as they could, they snagged the logs with the hook and pulled them out into the current where they could attach a choker line and tow them behind the boat.

THE DISTANCE

For several minutes, they were successful in grabbing logs. Until suddenly, with a violent jolt, the boat was struck on the side by a floating tree with branches still attached that were jerkily waving on the water surface. Both Wilbert and Hubert were ejected into the furious waters. They were submerged before they realized what had happened. Thomas struggled to regain control of the boat. He desperately threw a rope into the water, yelling, "Catch it, catch it!"

Both men were fighting to keep heads above water, gulping frantically, eyes bulging with terror. There was a pike pole lying in the bottom of the boat. Thomas pushed it towards Wilbert, who with his weak back, was the least able swimmer. Fortunately, Wilbert reached it and pulled himself forward, and then flipped, gasping, into the bottom of the boat. He struggled to pull himself up on the gunwale, choking and calling to Hubert.

Hubert, still flailing in the water, saw that Wilbert was in the boat and screamed, "Help, help!" as he frantically waved his arm. Wilbert, still barely able to breathe, reached as far over the gunwale as he could, but it wasn't far enough. He felt his heart thumping in his chest and couldn't take his eyes off Hubert's hand as it rose and sank, rose and sank.

Thomas again pushed the pike pole as far out as he could. Hubert could only grasp the slippery metal hook on the end but not keep it in his hand. The sharp hook, intended to stab logs, tore into his hand, and blood spurted forth. He cried in pain. "Help, help!" He again grabbed at the pole, then disappeared, and finally he was no longer above water.

Wilbert panted for oxygen, still crying out for Hubert, while Thomas struggled to believe what had happened. They both clung to the edge of the boat. The current pushed the boat out, and it began floating downstream. Thomas fought to restart the stubborn motor and manoeuvre the boat. He was able to direct it upstream along the shoreline as he tried to find the spot of the accident. The noise of the river splashing and churning pushed into their concentration as they desperately searched. There, lodged between the giant roots of an unstable tree, they glimpsed a patch of dark hair on the surface of the water.

Wilbert cried out, "I think I see something caught under the branch of that snag." Sure enough, Hubert's body moved listlessly in the bouncing water, eyes staring vacantly into space, no longer capable of seeing. "Get him in the boat fast. Maybe he's still alive," choked Wilbert. Thomas, with a grim face, nodded but knew that Hubert was not alive.

The task of getting the body back into the boat was almost insurmountable. The dead weight was unwieldy; loose limbs waved without intention. Wilbert's arms trembled with exhaustion. Finally, they were successful, and Hubert lay in a heap in the bottom of the boat. Both men fought back their horror and forced themselves to stare at the river ahead rather than their lifeless brother and partner. They had no energy to say anything to each other. Wilbert's mind raced with thoughts: *This is Thomas's fault. What will I do without Hubert? How can I tell our family?*

Thomas closed his mind to his nagging guilt and told himself that it wasn't his fault, that he'd done the best he could. At the same time, he faced the disturbing thought that it would be only the two of them working together from now on.

The trip to Hanna's ranch seemed to take an eternity. Of course Hanna knew what to do. He got a message to the wharf, and a boat was sent to Kaslo to report the drowning. Hubert's death was confirmed by the coroner the next day. Despite the obvious tension, Hanna helped the men make decisions. After wrapping the body in gunny sacks, they placed it carefully in Hanna's wagon, and the three of them drove slowly up the wagon trail to a high slope of Mount Willet. They chose a burial site, and Hanna left them to complete the task.

THE DISTANCE

Wilbert and Thomas worked methodically side by side to dig the grave and bury Hubert, always aware of the mountains' presence. Wilbert carved a small wooden cross and placed it on the mound of dirt. Each of the men said a silent prayer for Hubert.

Although overwhelmed with grief, Wilbert wrote to his family about Hubert's death.

My dear family,

Writing this letter is most difficult. Tears pour down my cheeks as I think of all of you. Your son and sibling, and my dear brother, has tragically passed away in a logging accident. The accident happened when we were working from a small boat, retrieving logs that were snarled in the edges of a riverbank.

The boat was very small and was not strong enough to cope with the churning currents in the river. It capsized, and both Hubert and I were thrown out. I was able to reach a pole and get back in the boat, but Hubert was not. Thomas and I, both in the boat, searched the riverbank until we found Hubert's body, however, we were too late to save him from drowning. We choked on our tears as we struggled to get his body back into the boat before going for help.

A neighbour assisted us to wrap Hubert's body and take him in the wagon to a burial spot high on the mountainside, where we dug a grave. I carved a small cross to mark his place.

29

Since Hubert made the decision to leave you and come along with me, he became more important to me every day. I'm sure that if he had stayed, he would have filled the same role for you. His faithfulness to his family members, his world experience, and his physical strength made him uniquely invaluable to each of us. I found his thoughtful advice to be a touchstone for me when we had to make difficult decisions.

I feel very guilty to have been a part in his death. If I had not shared my dreams with him and he had not been enticed to come, he would still be with you. I pray that you will forgive me and that we will all find peace in our hearts as we remember him.

Your loving son and brother,

Wilbert

Our dear Wilbert,

It is already six weeks since Hubert's death. Much as you suffered in writing the letter, we have suffered in reading it. Our hearts are broken. Thank you for the explanation of what happened and for describing the spot where he lies. We appreciate how well you cared for him after his death. If any of us are able to visit there in the future, please take us to pray over his grave. We will create a small memorial to his memory on our mantelpiece.

Please accept that we do not hold you responsible in any way for taking Hubert away from us or for the accident. We know from your letters to us that you were sharing the work together and made a good team. We are proud of both of you, our two sons. You did the best you could do, and Hubert would have done the same for you.

By the time you receive our letter another six weeks will have passed since the sad day. We hope that you are beginning to heal from such a difficult experience.

With much love,

Mama, Papa, and family

For a time, both Wilbert and Thomas were consumed with their inner confusion and sorrow. The task of writing letters to the family was extremely painful for Wilbert, although he never told Thomas about the exchange of letters and how distraught they were to learn of Hubert's death. Thomas found extra work to do for Hanna, which made it easy to avoid Wilbert at least temporarily.

However, after a couple of weeks, they knew that it was necessary to get back to their work. With heavy hearts, they continued the back-breaking labour of clearing land in the pre-emption, with only the two of them to share the load. Words between them were scarce and feelings constrained. Hubert's death was an almost impenetrable cloud of sadness, confusion, questioning, and suspicion. Both men were wracked with the guilt of failing their responsibility for Hubert, who had done his best to be a strong partner. And yet they worked, day after day, week after week, year after year. Tired and often discouraged, yet able to work side by side as a team, the men carried the ghost of Hubert on their shoulders forever.

*

HANS INTERRUPTED HARRY'S STORY. "How awful! How could they go on?"

"Hard to imagine, isn't it?" I agreed. "I suppose they had no choice."

Hans, with a pensive expression replied, "Hard to be so far away from the family at a time like that."

I answered, "Somebody at the trial told me that Wilbert received letters from his family in Switzerland who were horrified about the death of Hubert. Over the next two years, they put pressure on Wilbert to return to Switzerland. They felt a visit from him was urgent because he might not be able to get back home if war broke out in Europe, as was being predicted. In addition to their pressure, he realized the timing for a visit was good because he was beginning to agree with his family that it would be very useful to have a wife to share the home he was building. He was ready to have some companionship.

1914

~

In 1914, Wilbert returned to Neuchatel. He found it comfortable being home surrounded by familiar people who spoke French. His sisters had written that they knew a young woman, Liza, who worked in a bakery with them, and thought that she might be a very fine choice for a wife. Even though Liza was ten years younger than Wilbert, they were impressed with her maturity. According to Gertrude and Millie, she was friendly, helpful, and a hard worker. They also commented on how particular Liza was about her appearance. With hopes of sparking a potential marriage, members of both families arranged a picnic in the park, telling Liza that friends and family would also attend. Liza's parents, familiar with the Jeanneret family, gave her permission to join the gathering.

Liza, excited to go to the picnic, carefully chose a sky-blue summer dress that accentuated her periwinkle-blue eyes and tied her chestnut brown hair back with matching blue ribbons. Her sister, Harriet, introduced Wilbert to her and explained that he was visiting from Canada, where he had been living for a few years. From Liza's perspective, this was a perfect opportunity to chat and ask many questions.

"I have seen pictures of Canada. What is it like there?" questioned Liza in French.

Wilbert, taken aback by the intensity of her gaze, stumbled for words as he answered in French. "Well, it's big. With many trees and lakes and mountains." He was intrigued by her appearance and youth.

"Do they speak French?" asked Liza.

"Not much French, mostly English," replied Wilbert.

"Oh, I understand you speak English. I can't speak English at all." Wilbert listened and nodded.

"Do you live on a mountain? Do you have a house? Are there bears?" Liza had so many questions she didn't allow Wilbert time to answer.

"Yes to all those questions. I'm building a house. It's small because I don't have a family," said Wilbert, shifting his weight from one foot to the other with embarrassment.

"You must be lonely with no family around. Don't you miss your sisters?"

"I hope they will come for a visit when I'm more settled," replied Wilbert. "What I really miss is good baking like we have here."

Liza giggled and responded, "I should be more modest, but I make delicious breads and cakes. I work in the bakery with your sisters."

"Really!" said Wilbert. "I know they are excellent cooks."

Liza looked up at Wilbert shyly. "It sounds so interesting. I want to travel and see new places. I've heard of British Columbia before. One of my sisters lives in Spokane, and I've always wanted to go there."

Liza and Wilbert had a long conversation, oblivious to others, and by the end of the picnic, were smiling and laughing together. Wilbert was charmed by the enthusiasm of the young woman, and in spite of Wilbert's reticence and quietness, Liza was attracted to him because he gave full attention to her unceasing chatter. Also, she was delighted with ideas of a life in such a place as British Columbia, Canada.

THE DISTANCE

After several more visits in their respective family homes, Wilbert proposed to Liza, who was barely able to contain her excitement. Both families supported the match, and plans were made for a wedding.

ARRIVING AT LAST

~

Summer 1914

Liza's heart was thumping wildly. She was finally on the last leg of her remarkable journey from Europe to the wilds of Canada. She stood alone on the deck of the *Moyie* paddle steamer as it glided smoothly on Kootenay Lake. Her memories were tumbling over each other. Months ago, at home in Switzerland, she and Wilbert decided to marry. Members of both families approved of the marriage, and with much excitement, an elegant wedding was planned, and the wedding dress was made.

But then, after all the buildup, her world collapsed! The family learned that in Switzerland a girl was not allowed to be married until the age of eighteen, even with parental consent. So either they would need to wait six weeks until her birthday or get married in Canada. This was a problem for Wilbert who had commitments in BC and couldn't wait the six weeks in Switzerland to married. Another factor was that the political signs in Europe pointed to war being imminent, so they knew it was important to leave as soon as possible.

Fortunately, their church minister knew what to do and wrote to a ministerial colleague in Montreal to see if he would perform the wedding there. The minister agreed, and Wilbert went ahead to do business in Montreal while Liza stayed in Neuchatel making final preparations for her trip. She then travelled alone on the steamship, impatiently enduring the long voyage over the Atlantic Ocean to Canada. Many passengers spoke French so she was able to meet and chat with others, always having company at the dinner table.

In Montreal, she was relieved again to find that French was widely spoken so she didn't feel too much like a stranger. After the wedding, the next part of the trip was equally excruciating as she continued on her journey to British Columbia. Wilbert had gone ahead of her because Liza was first going to Spokane, U.S.A. to visit her sister and practise English. The train from Montreal to Spokane was tedious, as was the visit at sister Eleanor's place.

Eleanor had left Switzerland when Liza was in school, and they hardly knew each other; however, Liza was impressed with her good English. Every day they practised new words. "There are so many new things to think about, I find it hard to remember the words!" Liza commented with frustration.

"Let's go out for lunch, and I can help you tell the waiter your order. I'll tell you what to say. At least you know 'please' and 'thank you,'" replied Eleanor. After three weeks of tutoring from her sister and a few attempts to use English in public, Liza was still annoyed that she had learned only six words!

"I'm so grateful for your help, Eleanor. Maybe I'll learn faster when I'm with Wilbert," Liza said almost apologetically. When she left Spokane to go north over the border to Nelson, British Columbia, Eleanor pinned a note on her jacket that said, "I do not speak English."

Another slow train took her to Nelson, where she stayed the night in a hotel before boarding the sternwheeler ship that would take her to

THE DISTANCE

the north end of Kootenay Lake. Wilbert had told her about the long trip up the lake on the sternwheeler, so she knew it was the last part of her journey. She reassured herself in French, "I'll be in Argenta today. Wilbert will be at the dock waiting!" The long day ahead—at least seven hours on the ship—seemed like an eternity. She glanced sideways at the other passengers, wondering if anybody else spoke French and feeling shy about knowing only a few words of English. Liza missed chatting with all the people around her, being the gregarious person that she was.

The soft wool flannel of her long jacket felt soothing as she put her hands in her pockets. The square shoulders were shaped around wide lapels, the fashion in Europe. She loved the blue-grey tones of the fabric that so effectively set off her pristine white blouse with the silky lace high neckline. *Gramma's special gift for me on my journey*, she mused. Her slender body was evident beneath the graceful shape of the jacket as it extended to just above her knees with a long, loose matching skirt below. Low-heeled, lace-up shoes made up her ensemble, and she felt proud of her appearance. Her long chestnut hair was pulled into a simple bun at the nape of her neck, with a few tendrils escaping to frame her round, rosy cheeks. A small matching hat balanced perfectly on the top of her thick hair was held in place with long hat pins and decorated with a discreet yellow feather on one side. Her excitement vibrated through vivacious blue eyes. She felt the appreciative glances from other passengers and was pleased that she had dressed so carefully.

The *Moyie* gracefully made its way east on Kootenay Lake, following the west arm. Although she had a very early quick breakfast at the hotel, Liza was delighted to discover the ship had a dining room, complete with elegant table settings, fine dinnerware, and silver serving dishes. When the ship reached Balfour, where the west arm merged into the main lake, a luncheon was served much to Liza's pleasure, as the breakfast just wasn't enough. She gulped down the soup and boiled fish and rushed back out onto the upper deck. She didn't want to miss anything!

As the *Moyie* negotiated the currents and emerged from the Balfour narrows, the view of the main lake opened before her. Liza was awed at the wide expanse of water framed by mountains that stretched northward beyond sight. Vertical ridges tapered downward onto the beaches, and the peaks sparkled in the early summer sunlight. The depth of the cerulean sky was etched with swirling cirrus clouds.

The engines huffed and puffed a towering column of steam as the broad paddlewheel pulsed through the water, propelling the long ship northward. From her vantage point on the upper deck, Liza heard the splashing as the paddlewheel rotated through the pristine lake water with regularity. *The water smells so clean. Everything here seems so clean, so fresh.*

On the shore, she noticed strange buildings in a couple of places that seemed to have wooden chutes extending into the lake water below. She later learned these were mine sites, and the chutes were built for sending ore from higher up in the mine shaft to barges that travelled the lake.

The ship made a stop in the village of Kaslo to unload cargo and then set off northward again. In the distance was the sentinel Mount Willet, watchful guardian of the north and east ends of the lake and the overseer of "The Flats," the broad wetlands where the Duncan River merged into the lake. Liza gazed at the massive double peaks that sloped gracefully to the water's edge. Decades of avalanches had cut paths through the dense darkness of fir, cedar, hemlock, and larch. The snow-covered western peak jutted sharply forward. An almost horizontal ridge led to the broader, sturdy eastern peak, also encased in white.

As she absorbed the spectacular scene, she was reminded of a childhood trip to Lake Lucerne in Central Switzerland, where the combination of the broad lake and picturesque mountains had made a deep impression. The memory and the similarities were comforting to her as her uncertainties about her new life swirled in her mind.

The ship drew closer to the eastern shore. Rock cliffs dropped into the water, interspersed with pebble beaches and cedar driftwood logs that lay beached like the carcasses of deserted whales. Peering into one tiny bay, she caught sight of human habitation, the first since leaving Kaslo. She saw several teepees, and on the water's edge were sharp-nosed birch-bark canoes. Liza whispered to herself, "Is that a real Kootenai village?" She remembered Wilbert talking about the Kootenai people and their canoes on the beach.

The boat continued north and gently moved toward the shoreline. The soft breeze brought aromatic scents of the forest, with a damp essence of fir and cedar, occasionally noticeable even over the whiffs of exhaust. Bald eagles circled above the trees on the shore and then perched on the treetops, silently watching. An osprey hovered over the lake and dive-bombed into the water, wings flailing, then popped out and pushed itself upward, talons gripping a writhing fish.

One of the eagles spotted an easy target for dinner and screeched from its post to intercept the osprey. The air battle began. Both birds dipped and dived as they evaded each other. The eagle grasped at the fish hanging beneath the osprey with its talons, and with a sudden lurch, the struggling fish was freed, splashing into the lake. The birds circled each other once more and then returned to roost. The show was over. Liza, awestruck, thought, *I have never seen anything like that in Switzerland!*

Bringing her view back to the base of the goliath mountain, she saw a dock and people with horses and wagons obviously waiting for the ship. The broad end of the dock was stacked with materials ready to load on

JUDY POLLARD

the boat. Sturdy pilings held the dock and the wide ramps in place and were built to resist the fiercest wind storms the lake could offer.

The whistle sounded a greeting, and the *Moyie* slowly eased up beside the dock and was skillfully positioned with the front-loading door open to the platform. The dock was only large enough to allow space for the open loading doors, approximately the front quarter of the boat. The back of the long ship extended far behind. Above, the tall stack continued to release a column of white smoke. The noise of the boat quieted. Liza was relieved because she wanted to take in the sounds and smells of the lake and the beach and the activity before her. She felt her anticipation increasing as she watched impatiently while the crew jumped across the narrow space to drag heavy hemp ropes and wrap them around large capstans, strong enough to hold the ship in rough waters. The surface gently bobbed with the motion of the ship. Finally, the ship's ramp was lowered, and the captain instructed everybody to disembark.

Liza gingerly stepped down the gangplank as she searched the faces of people for her husband. Her mind was racing. *Where is he? He promised to meet me. How will I know where to go in this impossible place? No streets, only a dirt wagon track.* Excitement began to turn to panic. As she pushed her way between people noisily greeting each other and saying farewell to those departing, tears began to trickle down her cheeks. Not paying attention to the traffic, she was bumped by a wheelbarrow pushing a load from the ship, which caused her to trip and fall. Embarrassed, she struggled to get up and hoped nobody noticed. *Is that a hand? Someone is helping me.* Liza looked up into Wilbert's face blubbering in French, "You are here. I was so scared." She burst into tears as Wilbert wrapped his arms around her.

"Of course, you should have more confidence in me," he muttered as his twinkling eyes searched hers. They held each other, happy to finally

42

THE DISTANCE

be together again, and kissed shyly, aware of the curious looks surrounding them.

Taking command, Wilbert said, "Let's find your trunk and get in the wagon." He pushed past the people crowding around the luggage, as he looked for her distinctive camelback wooden trunk wrapped in its bands of metal. Liza waited, watching with anxious eyes. She couldn't see it anywhere. Nobody else had a solid oak trunk like hers with a curved top and two hasps on the front securely fixed with locks. She knew the trunk had a large label on the top with her name.

"It came safely to Spokane! Where is it now?" she said to Wilbert, tugging on his arm. Just as they were about to go back into the ship storage area and search, a worker appeared pushing a wheelbarrow. In it was the trunk! Wilbert directed him to take the heavy wheelbarrow up the long ramp to the shore and put the trunk into the waiting wagon. Liza followed, catching her breath as she watched the men. The horses stood patiently, ignoring Liza. Moving to stand in front of them, Liza commented, "These are sturdy horses. What are their names?"

"Ya, they're draught horses. Bert and Bessie. Bessie sometimes gets impatient and cranky with Bert. You'll find that out when you get to know them," replied Wilbert as he took her hand and helped her climb onto the seat of the wagon.

Liza giggled. "I love horses but never had the chance to get to know any before."

Wilbert finally got up onto the seat, took the reins, and commanded the horses to walk. Liza breathed a heavy sigh. "Oh, I'm so relieved. I was terrified the trunk my uncle Peter made for me had disappeared just when I was almost here. Where do we go now? Wilbert, will you take me to the home you promised?"

Steering the horses toward the narrow track up the mountainside, Wilbert smiled at her reassuringly. "You must be patient. We'll get there soon," he said. He then snapped the reins and urged the horses to move faster up the steepening path. The pace quickened, and the wagon bounced along through ruts and holes and over rocks. The thick forest alongside the path created shadows that seemed impenetrable. Liza breathed deeply as she took in the richness of the air around her, and she marvelled at the wildness compared to her home in Switzerland. As the track steepened, the horses slowed to a pause. The path had flattened out at the top of the steep drop, and the valley bottom could be seen below.

"Listen, Wilbert, I can hear a whispering wind in the tops of those tall trees beside us. They sound like they're talking to each other." Wilbert grunted in response and urged the horses forward. Wilbert and Liza sat close together on the narrow bench and their shoulders rubbed in unison with the jiggling of the wagon. Soon they would be at their home.

As they travelled along, Liza looked at Wilbert beside her. Broad-shouldered, strong, and stocky, he was not much taller than her. And she had already learned of his frequent silence. She felt safe with him, even in such a foreign place. As usual, his woollen pants were held up with thick black suspenders. She detected the smell of sweat and dirt. His shirt looked rumpled under the tweed jacket, as if in need of a good wash and iron. A cap was jammed on his head and covered his dark, greasy-looking hair sticking out below the edges. She knew there would be a lot of cleaning to get him and his clothing in better shape! *What will our home be like?* she wondered.

"Wilbert, tell me, how much farther? I can't see anything but trees, and you won't tell me . . ." she chattered. He, as usual, looked quietly at her, pipe in his mouth, and gave a wry smile. He wanted her to be surprised, so he wasn't revealing any secrets.

THE DISTANCE

The steepness of the path lessened, and the track turned a sharp corner, leading toward an opening in the forest. Liza strained to see farther and wished Wilbert would go faster. Suddenly they were in brilliant sunlight and in full view of the gentle slope with a clearing on the hillside. It was obvious that many trees had recently been cut, as stumps dotted the space.

Liza was astonished to see a square, compact house built in the neat, orderly style of houses in her hometown. The windows on the upper floor were placed exactly over the windows on the lower floor. Light curtains could be seen fluttering in the breeze. "Is this our house?" She threw her arms around his shoulders and nearly pushed him off the wagon seat, saying, "Stop, stop, let me get down." Jumping to the ground, she got tangled in her skirts but struggled free and raced to the doorway. Wilbert got out of the wagon and, with no apparent haste, began to unload her wooden trunk and carry it to the door, remaining silent though a slight smile played on his lips.

Liza danced from one foot to the other, waiting for the door to be opened. Wilbert gently pushed past her and pushed it aside. Rushing in, she exclaimed in astonishment, "The kitchen is like home!" She clasped her hands in delight as she admired the magnificent iron cook stove with its coal-black smooth top, the shiny metal edges, the clean, untarnished circular plates, the large warming oven above the main surface, and even a tank on the side to heat water. Throwing her arms around him, she asked, "How did you find this for me? I can hardly wait to cook dinner!" She noticed the hand pump for drawing water in the corner, with a bucket placed underneath. "Is there not running water at the sink? I see a bucket under the sink."

45

"I apologize. Not yet, but it will be built as soon as I can purchase the materials so the water will run out of the sink and into a pipe and be drained outside," explained Wilbert. "The work is simple."

"Oh, I'm glad. Now I want to see the other rooms." She rushed through an open doorway into small, tidy parlour, with one chair and a settee near the window. A pot-bellied wood stood in the corner. Liza turned toward Wilbert, obviously ready to keep exploring.

Wilbert mumbled that he hadn't been able to get more furniture yet. "Come see the bedroom," he said. He took her hand and led her into an equally small, plain room with a carefully made-up bed. She suspected that detail of tidiness to be in her honour and giggled. Wilbert encased her in his arms and smothered her with kisses on her face, her neck, her lips. He was immersed in her sweet perfume and the softness of her skin.

Liza, suddenly uncertain, wriggled herself free. "I need my trunk so I can change. Where's the bathroom?"

He opened a side door and pointed to the outhouse twenty feet away. "I'll build us a bathroom when I can. There is a tub I'll bring into the kitchen to use for a bath," he said with a shy glance. Liza looked at him with disbelief. Confused by her reaction, he returned to the entrance and retrieved her trunk from the doorstep. He put it carefully on the table in the bedroom so she could easily unpack and put her things in the closet and bureau.

Liza stood waiting, wondering what to do next, again feeling the awkwardness of their wedding night in the hotel in Montreal. Emotions flooded her as she remembered her home in Switzerland and thought about living with Wilbert in the first bedroom of their own, in this house in the wilds of Canada.

BUILDING A LIFE TOGETHER

~

Wilbert and Liza gradually settled into their new existence together. Each morning, they woke with the first light. Wilbert quietly went to the kitchen and lit the stove, putting the kettle on the spot to heat it most quickly for tea. Liza sleepily stretched and crawled out of bed, pulling her robe over her nightdress and sliding her feet into woollen slippers. She found the floors cold even in early summer.

By the time she got to the kitchen, Wilbert had put out the breakfast plates and jam. It was delicious strawberry jam, a gift from the Hanna family. Liza thought, *Next summer I'll grow strawberries and start raspberry bushes in our little garden. I love making jam.* After the frying pan was heated, Liza made eggs for each of them while she carefully put the toast in the wire rack, watching it so she could turn it over before it burned.

Breakfast was always a bright part of the day for them; it was a relaxed and comfortable time. The table was in front of the window, and the view of the small clearing in front of the house was busy with birds and squirrels, flitting and chasing each other in the bright sunlight. Liza excitedly chattered and pointed at a pileated woodpecker, not recognizing it as a bird she'd seen back home.

"What a colourful bird. So majestic!"

Wilbert mumbled, "Not so majestic when it hammers holes into the cracks in the walls to dig out bugs. Can do damage, that bird!"

"Just the same, it's beautiful. Where are you working today?"

"Still making enough space for our barn. See those trees over there? They come down next. I only have two weeks to work near the house before Thomas and I go back to do more clearing for an orchard area. I want to get as much done here as I can, then we'll be ready to start building a barn."

Breakfast over, Wilbert put on his boots, went to the shed, picked up his axe and saw, and then went to meet Thomas, who was waiting outside. Although Liza had met Thomas shortly after she arrived, she realized she knew very little about him. Wanting to learn more, she decided to invite Thomas to dinner for a proper conversation.

Each day was filled with continuous work. Thomas had purchased some dynamite to blow out tree stumps, so Wilbert was eager to try removing stumps in the clearing by the house. However, he hadn't told Liza about it yet. He thought Liza would be nervous about them using dynamite because she knew it was being used for bombs in the war in Europe.

After clearing up the breakfast, Liza baked fresh bread and rolls in the kitchen range—superb delicacies. *This is the best present Wilbert could ever give me! He is a thoughtful husband, although always thinking about work.* She mused as she cleaned up the bedroom, remembering the nights with Wilbert. *Will I ever stop being so shy when he tries to touch me? I'm nervous. He tells me he doesn't want to hurt me. I don't know what I'm supposed to do. If my sister were here, she would tell me . . . she has a husband.*

It was mail day. Before lunch, she walked to the wharf to meet the *Moyie*, singing loudly to alert any wildlife in the area. As she journeyed

THE DISTANCE

down the hill, she marvelled at the land around her. The mountains changed with the shadows as the sun caught them here and there, and she had noticed that at dusk they became mysteriously higher and blacker. The huge mass of Mount Willet was dense, and the peaks were brilliantly snowy in the sun. *What a magical world to be surrounded by such beauty. And it feels like the mountain is protecting me even though it is such a distance from my first home.* She was excited to see a letter in the mail from Wilbert's sister in Switzerland. She hurried home up the steep wagon road to show it to Wilbert when he came in for lunch.

"There's a letter, Wilbert. It's from Rose. She'll be here in two weeks! I need to prepare the guest room for her, and we need to find another bed. I'll go to town and get fabric to make nice curtains and covers. Do you think the neighbours, the Filipeks, might have a bed we could borrow for now?"

Wilbert, astonished that his sister was coming to visit so soon, groaned inwardly about the interference in his work, until he realized that Liza going to town for a day was the perfect opportunity to try the dynamite on the stumps in the field. "Guess we have a lot of work to do," he agreed. "I'll talk to the neighbours about borrowing a bed."

The next days were busy with preparing everything to create a pleasant guest room to impress Rose. Liza went to Kaslo on the *Moyie* to shop, and Wilbert and Thomas successfully removed stumps with the dynamite. When Liza returned, the job was almost finished, and Wilbert explained to her how quickly the dynamite had cleared the stumps out and made it easier to prepare the space to build the barn. Liza, pleased after the successful shopping trip, forgot about how dangerous the dynamite was, much to the relief of Wilbert because he knew there would be more dynamiting in the future weeks and years. After all, it was the most effective method of removing the stumps.

49

When Rose arrived, Liza was surprised at her height, her buxom appearance, and her jolly, outgoing nature. They had only met once several years before in Switzerland when Liza was much younger. Rose was eight years older than Wilbert, and when Wilbert and Liza were planning the wedding, Rose was living in Geneva so she couldn't join the family.

"Wilbert, it's so good to see you again. And Liza, you look different. I never would have recognized you," exclaimed Rose when she was greeted at the dock by Liza and Wilbert. "You were still a girl when I first met you."

Wilbert gave Rose a tentative peck on each cheek as he smiled his welcome. I'm glad you came to see our new home."

Rose looked around and commented, "There is nothing here but trees and mountains. I'm looking forward to seeing your house."

"Well we'll go up the mountain to our house right away," reassured Wilbert. He picked up Rose's luggage and put it in the wagon while Liza walked with Rose and stood beside her as she climbed up the step onto the wagon seat. "Sorry it's such a big step," she apologized to Rose. Our wagon is very old and plain."

As they rode in the wagon, bouncing over the ruts and rocks, Rose commented on the thickness of the bushes and trees and the lack of people. Don't you miss seeing people?"

Liza explained that the days were full of work. "We're building our barn and clearing space for the garden. And I've been adding a woman's touch in the house. The neighbours are friendly, but they live a distance away. Sometimes we hear their dogs bark but not often."

Rose leaned forward to look at a path going off the wagon road and asked, "Where does that go?"

THE DISTANCE

"That's the short path to our closest neighbour. I hope to take you to visit them while you're here," responded Liza, "and we'll go to Hubert's grave soon. We miss Hubert. He was a good brother and a hard worker. Thomas, Wilbert's partner, visits us a lot because he's all by himself. He's coming for dinner tomorrow so you'll get a chance to meet him."

Rose brightened up immediately, eager to socialize after the long trip. "Is he the one who was in the Swiss Guard? Wilbert told me about him. I'd like to meet him."

The next morning, Liza and Rose decided to prepare traditional Swiss food for the dinner with Thomas. A favourite was always rosti—hash-browned potatoes with onions and bacon and lots of melted cheese on top. The bacon was a special treat that Rose had brought from home. It was more flavourful than the bacon they sometimes purchased in Kaslo, and so it was greatly enjoyed, especially by Wilbert.

The next morning, after visiting Hubert's grave, Liza suggested to Rose that they go for a walk in the forest and find some mushrooms to add as well. It took only a few minutes to spot the deeply wrinkled, dark, cone-shaped tops of the morel mushrooms poking through the detritus on the forest floor and show them to Rose. Rose noticed several more mushrooms right in front of her. "Look at them all. They look like a miniature forest!" Their bucket was soon filled.

Thomas arrived with exuberant greetings. His thick, dark hair and mysterious, coal-black eyes were pleasing, and his easy composure and wit were appealing. Rose was impressed with the tall, muscular man. She was ready for something new and interesting in her life.

Rose insisted that Thomas sit beside her for dinner. When Thomas realized the dinner was rosti, he exclaimed, "Like food at home! It smells delicious. And what are those small, dark things?"

51

"They're morel mushrooms," explained Rose. "Liza taught me where to find them this morning. And we cooked them in butter. How do you like them?"

Thomas ate hungrily, nodding with enjoyment. "I haven't tasted food like this since I came to Canada."

She caught his eye and smiled. "You must be eating some good food. You're so strong to work in the woods every day. Wilbert told me you were in the Swiss Guard."

Thomas brushed his hand against Rose's arm and answered. "That was back in Switzerland. The work here is much harder. But I don't have to carry a gun with me all the time. Except for the times when there are signs of a bear or a cougar in the area!"

Rose's warm attention and flirtatiousness affected Thomas, and he responded by inviting her to accompany him. "Would you like to come up the mountain tomorrow? I will bring my rifle in case we meet wild animals."

Rose's face lit up with pleasure, and she assured him that she would be delighted to go and, of course, she would feel safe with him.

After four short weeks, in which Rose and Thomas spent more and more time together, Rose returned home to Switzerland. By that time, the two had decided to marry within a year. Arrangements were made for Rose and Thomas to meet in Montreal the following spring to be married, after which they would return to Argenta. Before spring, Thomas managed to finish building a substantial log house on his property on the flats.

He boasted to Wilbert, "Look at the smoothly peeled logs and perfectly shaped tongue and groove joints!"

Wilbert nodded in agreement that the workmanship was superb while being somewhat surprised that Thomas had become skilled at log

THE DISTANCE

house building. Thomas was clearly focused on getting the job done and impressing Rose.

By the time Thomas travelled to Montreal for the wedding, the house was well-prepared and when they returned as a married couple, Rose was delighted. A baby girl was born before the end of the year. Liza was somewhat envious because she regretted that she hadn't yet become pregnant. Although satisfied that she and Wilbert were diligently involved in the arduous work of clearing land and building their property, she felt the lack of children.

Liza commented to Wilbert, "Did you know Rose was pregnant? I didn't know it could happen that fast." Wilbert shrugged his shoulders, seeming to be more interested in reading than talking.

1916

~

After two years of living in Argenta, Liza, at twenty years old, was strong and slender, a vivacious young woman, with flowing brown hair now naturally highlighted by the sun as she worked outside for hours daily. Her complexion glowed with lightly tanned skin and coloured cheeks, showing off her bright blue eyes. The seasons enthralled her, and she looked forward to the shifts from summer to fall to winter to spring. She enjoyed the varying angles of the sunlight on the mountainside and the fresh fragrances of the air.

Winter in Argenta was different from Switzerland. In Argenta, there was snow and cold, but the weather could be very changeable. When a storm started, it would snow and snow for a few days, and then get warmer and suddenly change to rain. It might rain for four or five days without stopping and melt the snow, creating flooding creeks and washed-out wagon roads. When the weather changed again, the ground would freeze into ridges and lumps, making a wagon ride rough and uncomfortable.

During the storms of winter, Wilbert and Liza continued to build the inside of the barn since the roof and side walls were completed. They were happy with their progress, and Liza began looking for another cow to buy so she could sell milk, cream, and butter. She began asking the neighbours if they knew of any milk cows for sale. Liza finally found a cow to buy from the Filipeks and began selling extra milk, butter, and cheese. Back home in Switzerland, she had become an expert cheesemaker, and her delicious products were now popular with her neighbours.

Whenever new people moved into the community, Liza took them a gift of cheese to welcome them, explaining that she knew what it felt like to be a newcomer. Liza understood that the newest neighbours, Mr. and Mrs. Vadas, were from Germany and spoke little English. It was fortunate that she spoke some German because one of her relatives was German-Swiss. When she went to greet them, she introduced herself in German to their surprise and delight. Sylvie Vadas was Liza's age, and the two young women began to accompany each other on the walk to the wharf on mail days. The two of them practised English together and became close friends. Liza's cheese continued to be a special treat for the Vadases because it tasted like the style of cheese from their home in Germany.

Mail day was the best chance for Liza to chat with neighbours without seeming too nosy. One day, Liza was by herself and even though she understood English better, she was still shy about starting conversations. She stood near three women who were whispering around the corner of the mail shed. Liza desperately tried to hear what they were saying. Mrs. Hanna, who had befriended Liza, sounded afraid. Her usually soft, dark eyes looked alarmed, and her smooth forehead was wrinkled in a deep frown. "Red McLeod," she said, and then repeated the name, "Red McLeod. Mr. Filipek said he saw him on the trail up Hamill Creek."

Liza heard gasps. "Really?"

Mrs. Hanna nodded vehemently. "It was definitely him!"

Liza didn't know the other women, but she could hear their consternation. One of them stated, "My husband says he's a drunken horse thief, always up to no good."

The other woman, looking shocked, exclaimed, "You mean there's a criminal here? What does he look like?"

"My husband told me to watch out for him," said Mrs. Hanna. "He's got a mane of hair the colour of carrot and rides a tall, grey horse. His penetrating intense blue eyes intimidate, and he towers over most of the men here. He sounds Scottish. The Mounties from Fort Steele can't seem to catch him. A devious trickster for sure."

The other woman, who was named Beryl, agreed. "I heard that he steals a horse or chicken from a farmyard, then goes to another farmer and offers to sell the animal and pockets the cash. Then he steals the same animal again and takes it back to the first owner, saying he found it and would sell it back to him, making even more profit!"

When Liza got home, she confronted Wilbert. "You didn't tell me about this man, Red McLeod! The women say he's been seen here, and he is huge!"

Wilbert, in his cautious way, looked at Liza and smiled. He pulled the curved pipe from his mouth and patted her hand. "Nothing to worry about. Thomas said he heard the police caught him in Duncan City."

"Have you ever seen him?"

"Only one time. I went past the cabin on the beach, and I saw him outside. He stayed there sometimes before he went up the Hamill Creek pass."

"Tell me what he looked like," said Liza, impatient with Wilbert's lack of concern. "Don't you know he's a criminal?"

"He's big all right, and so is his horse. Lots of red hair and a thick beard. The police finally have him in hand, so no need to worry," reassured Wilbert. But then he quietly mumbled under his breath, "Unless he tricks them and gets away again." Fortunately, Liza didn't hear his comment as she went in the kitchen to begin cooking dinner.

One day in early fall, as Liza was carrying buckets of milk from the barn, she noticed a strange popping sound above the house. She could see sparks spurting from the stovepipe onto the roof. Spots of flame were appearing. She yelled, "Wilbert! Fire!" By the time he appeared around the corner of the house, the smoke was becoming more acrid and flames were leaping.

"Go to the neighbours for help!" he shouted.

She raced to the nearest house and asked Mrs. Filipek to ring the emergency alarm on the party line phone. Soon neighbours were rushing to help put out the fire. Wilbert frantically dragged furniture out of the house, but it was too late. The fire viciously destroyed their home. They stood aghast in front of the demolished house, thick nauseating smoke curling around their bodies. They clung to each other, distraught to see how their fortunes could change so rapidly. They had no place to live other than the barn. After all their efforts to build a home, now most of their belongings were destroyed! Liza felt devastated and even suggested to Wilbert that they should return to Switzerland. Wilbert bleakly stared at the black pile and moaned, "No we can't. We stay here. We'll figure it out."

That evening, Thomas and Rose invited Wilbert and Liza for dinner and offered to let them live in their house. "You are very generous," said Liza. "I'm still trying to stop crying. We do appreciate your help." Wilbert despondently agreed that it was the best option. Within a few days, Liza and Wilbert had retrieved the furniture that had been thrown from the burning house and moved in with Rose and Thomas.

THE DISTANCE

*

"Seems to me that it must have been a blow to Wilbert's pride to pick up what was left and move in with Thomas, even if he was against the wall," I commented to Hans. "He was sensitive about people thinking he wasn't strong because of his humped back and, in spite of that, he was fiercely self-reliant and independent. He was a man of few words, so he probably didn't say much despite this adding to his sense of inferiority to Thomas. And he still had to be supportive to Liza. He couldn't even start thinking about a new house."

*

Liza was charmed by the year-old baby, Louise. She softly sang nursery rhymes in French and dreamed about having her own baby to cuddle and love. Rose was happy to have help with Louise and the never-ending work. During the winter months, baby Louise became more active—walking, climbing, and enjoying having people chase her. Rose appreciated Liza's quickness to retrieve Louise from trouble. As the days passed, Rose began to feel more tired and drained. She hadn't expected a baby to be so much work, and she began to be envious of Liza's energy and attractiveness.

Spring 1917

~

Spring finally arrived, and they could spend time outside on the grass. Liza found a soft ball to play with much to Louise's pleasure. Rose was more relaxed, with Louise being agreeable to rest at naptime after exerting herself chasing the ball. One day when Louise was asleep, Rose suggested, "Now I can try out the new washer machine that Wilbert's sisters sent to us from Switzerland. It takes two people to operate. Let's try it."

The two women stood in the yard and stared at the strange contraption. There was a large round barrel made of wooden staves bound by metal straps and supported on four legs. Rose tugged at the lever that looked like a broom handle, which was attached to the side of the barrel. "It moves if I push it hard. It's attached to a stem sticking up in the centre of the lid on the barrel."

Liza, peering into the hole in the lid of the barrel, said, "I can see something moving in there. I'm taking the lid off."

With the lid open, they could see the stem that protruded from the top was part of a large wooden agitator that turned back and forth when the handle was pushed forward and back. Liza found a bucket and began filling the barrel with water from the nearby stream flowing through the garden. "This is exhausting! That barrel is only half full. How about you

61

have a turn?" Eventually they agreed there was enough water to cover the items they wanted to put in, so Rose shaved the edge of a bar of lye soap into the water, and Liza threw in some sheets and towels for the first load of laundry.

"Who gets the first turn pushing the handle?" questioned Liza, catching Rose's eye. Taking the challenge, Rose immediately began working the handle. In the meantime, Liza inspected the other strange part of the machine. A ladder-like wooden apparatus, a foot and a half wide, stood at the back above the barrel. The bottom "rung" contained two long rollers, one above the other, and protruding from the side of the frame was a long handle. About two feet above the rollers, the top of the apparatus had two cross bars with a metal clamp on each corner.

"What is this?" questioned Liza.

Sweat already running down her face, Rose stopped pushing the lever and looked. "I saw that in Neuchatel before I came here. My aunt called it a wringer. You turn the handle and the rollers rotate. I watched her use it. First you pull a piece of laundry out of the tub, then push it through the wringer while you turn the handle at the same time. She was good at it. And I remember she had a big tub of clean water behind the washer machine so the clothes would fall from the wringer into the water and soap would be rinsed off."

"Should we try?" asked Liza. Rose pushed the lid off the barrel and dragged out a soaking wet sheet that felt as heavy as a bale of hay. She tried to push it toward the wringer while Liza turned the handle. It slipped and dropped back into the water, splashing Rose.

"Oh! Something's wrong," said Liza. "I'll try twisting those knobs on top. Maybe they push down and make the wringers tighter."

Grabbing a smaller towel from the water, Rose tried again to push it into the wringer while Liza turned the handle. Pushing forward with both hands, her face contorted, and she shrieked, "My fingers are caught! Stop turning!" just as the towel splashed back into the barrel. Rose jerked her fingers out, rubbing them frantically to get circulation back and glared at Liza through long pieces of her hair that now masked a soaked face.

"I'm sorry. I didn't see your hands there!" Liza exclaimed, resisting the urge to giggle. "I'll take the next turn." They switched places, and when her fingers became dangerously close to entrapment in the wringer, Liza pulled back hard and flopped onto her back on the ground, shocked and giggling.

Rose chortled as she helped Liza get up. "Maybe we should stick with the scrub board."

After a few more tries, they were able to make the items go through the wringer and fall into the large tub of water that they had filled and placed behind the washer. With sheets and towels in the rinse water, the next challenge was how to get them into the wringer and squeeze the water out before hanging them on the line.

They found that if they poured the water from the rinse tub, then lifted the laundry into the barrel that had been drained of water, they could pull the items up and push them through the wringer. Liza tried pushing a sheet through the wringer and turning the handle at the same time. Her whole hand was swallowed by the wringer before she realized it and stopped turning the handle. "Yikes! My hand is stuck." She tugged hard once, then twice, and got it out before Rose could help. "It's a devouring demon," Liza blurted out. They looked at each other in disbelief and dissolved into giggles.

Finally, the laundry was on the clothesline, the water was drained from the tubs, and the yard was drying in the warm sun. Rose and Liza, both dishevelled and drenched, collapsed in the kitchen to have lunch before Louise woke from her morning sleep. They agreed there would be a good story to tell the husbands that evening. "Maybe we can get a nap before they get back," muttered Rose.

Summer 1917

~

As the days turned into summer, the mosquitoes became a cloak of torment every time a person went outside. Loudly buzzing, they sharply penetrated thin clothing and created mountains of itchy lumps wherever they could. Liza complained to Wilbert, "I can't stand it. When I scratch the itching is like hot pokers. I can't sleep!"

Wilbert, who wasn't as susceptible to the mosquitoes as Liza, listened to her complaints and commented, "When the Kootenai people come from the south end of the lake, they bring dried yarrow flowers to rub on their skin. Keeps mosquitoes away."

"I want some of that. Will they come soon?"

"Ya. They come in the spring when the rainbow trout start going up the river to spawn. They catch a lot of fish."

Liza, determined to keep Wilbert talking, commented, "People at the wharf were talking about the abundance of berries. There are so many gooseberries and thimbleberries and Oregon grape and the Kootenai people will be coming to pick them. Apparently, they're especially fond of strawberries. There will be a group camped on the beach soon."

Wilbert looked up from his paper and said, "You'll see the pointed canoes and teepees when you go to the wharf."

65

"I think I saw some canoes like that when I first came here on the *Moyie*," commented Liza. "Why do they have the points on the ends?"

His attention finally brightened as Wilbert described one of his favourite observations, "Some people call them sturgeon-nosed canoes and say the shape is like the giant sturgeon fish that live in Kootenay Lake. They are rarely seen because they are bottom feeders. Those fish are highly valued by the Kootenai people," answered Wilbert.

"Have you ever seen one?" queried Liza.

"I've only seen one once since I came here. I was standing on a point where the water was only six or eight feet deep, and the sturgeon came close to shore. It looked like a dinosaur fish with ridges all down it's back and a pointed nose. It was as long as my wagon! Never seen anything like it."

"That's amazing," gasped Liza. "I hope I'll see one someday."

The very next time Liza walked to the wharf from the flats—well protected from mosquitoes with a hat, scarf, and long garments—she saw more people around the dock than usual. She saw many canoes pulled up on the beach. Nearby were several teepees with tall posts that created a cone shape, and large animal hides stretching over each other. At the top, there was a chimney hole, allowing wisps of smoke to escape. Men and women worked together to set up the camp, shaking out blankets, holding poles steady for the tents, and gathering firewood. Children of various sizes pitched in, carrying smaller logs and rocks to help build the fires.

Liza stood, entranced by the scene, before she noticed a woman walking over the rocky beach toward the wharf. The energetic strength of her body portrayed smooth power. Liza could imagine her moving through thick trees, never stumbling or hesitating, so sure was her step. Her arms swung at her sides. On her back was a sort of pack. Liza could

THE DISTANCE

see a strap wrapped on the tops of the woman's arms and around to the front of the chest. *That must be the cradle pack Mrs. Hanna told me she had seen once. I can see a baby bouncing along, watching the children running behind.*

The woman stepped up onto the wharf beside Liza. Her black hair was pulled back from her face, and her eyes were set deeply above high cheekbones. Small lips in a cautious smile conveyed a friendly greeting. Liza smiled and said, "Hello." The response was a slight nod.

Liza timidly peeked around at the baby in the cradle, and the woman, obviously proud of her little one, turned so that Liza could fully admire, grin at, and greet the baby with a small wave. The cradle on her back was skillfully crafted of bent willow, while the cover was made of buckskin and lined with rabbit fur. The outer edge was decorated with beads and feathers. Liza hesitantly touched the fur as she smiled at the baby, grateful that the mother was receptive and even encouraging.

Mrs. Hanna came to greet the woman and spoke a few words in a language that Liza didn't understand. "This is Malyan," she explained to Liza. She pointed to Liza and said her name to the woman. Mrs. Hanna grinned at the baby in the cradle and was greeted with a gurgle. Malyan drew a pouch from inside her deerskin shirt and offered it to Mrs. Hanna, who in return gave her a bag of flour from her pack. The exchange was made with little talking; however, both women looked satisfied.

Liza stood quietly watching and listening, wishing that she could speak better English, let alone their language. *Maybe Mrs. Hanna could teach me some words so I could make friends with Malyan.*

She asked Mrs. Hanna, "What is in the pouch?"

"Dried yarrow herb. Have you heard of it? It helps to keep mosquitoes away."

Liza excitedly responded, "Wilbert told me about it. He said if you rub it on your skin, mosquitoes don't land. I hate mosquitoes!"

"I thought you would be having a hard time with the mosquitoes. They're especially bad on the flats," commented Mrs. Hanna. "Have this pouch. Try mixing the dried herb with a little water and rubbing it on the bare skin of your face, neck, hands, and arms."

"Thank you so much. I will use it. When do the Kootenai people return?" asked Liza.

"They usually come in late summer when the redfish are running at the mouth of the Duncan River. The salmon in the lake begin to turn red when they're ready to spawn, so that's why they're called redfish. Many fish are caught, and they trade some with us. Then all of us have a supply of fish to dry and preserve for the winter. They are delicious fish, fat and red!" explained Mrs. Hanna.

"I love fish, so I hope to try some. And maybe by the time they return, I will learn a few words in their language," said Liza. "I hope you can help me. Thanks again for the yarrow."

After waving good-bye to the baby and Malyan, she raced back to Rose and Thomas's home to try the herb. She discovered that it worked so well she didn't need to wear big hats and long sleeves when outside. The mosquitoes stayed away! *What a relief, especially on the hot days! Maybe I can tolerate living on the flats for a while longer. Why don't the mosquitoes bother Rose or Wilbert or Thomas?*

Another mail day, and this time Liza was well covered with yarrow paste as she walked along the road. She loved to see the neighbours crowded on the wharf waiting for the *Moyie*. Her English was finally strong enough that she was comfortable chatting with people.

Maybe there was a letter or a package! Liza waited patiently for the mail to be sorted. She was delighted when the postmaster handed her

THE DISTANCE

a letter from Switzerland. It was a relief to read that her family was safe in their small Swiss town because the news they saw in the Kaslo newspaper described horrible stories about the Great War in Europe. Apparently, her family was able to produce vegetables and poultry to feed themselves, and there was not active fighting near them.

After reading the letter, Liza started the two-mile walk back to the house. She smiled to herself as she thought about the new skills she had learned in recent years. She knew her mother would be pleased at the new sewing skills. Today she was wearing a favourite green dress that she had made from fabric her mother had sent. It had a fitted bodice with round buttons up the front and a modest neckline. The sleeves were slender with buttons on the cuffs. Below the waist, the loose skirt flowed softly as she moved quickly down the narrow road that curved along the edge of the slough on the flats.

She skipped along the road, cheerfully singing "Frère Jacques," one of her favourite childhood songs, just as she always did when she was alone. It made her feel as if her mother was walking along with her. The dense green brush crowded the edge of the road and dripped with the moisture of the early morning showers. Monarch butterflies danced from branch to branch, displaying the bright yellow of their wings elegantly framed with sharp, black lines. It was a perfect day!

She slowed near the giant rock, named 'turtle rock' by the locals. The spot provided a good view to enjoy the view of the duck pond below the road. Suddenly she was aware of a presence emerging from the darkness of the mountain path just ahead. Her head jerked around. A tall, dark horse loomed above her. The rider looked gigantic. She heard a deep voice with a Scottish accent. "Hello lassie, and who might you be?"

Liza jumped back in alarm as the man leapt off the horse, holding the reins in his right hand, and stood in front of her, towering over her by at least a foot. Her mind was racing. At the wharf, she had heard someone whisper that Red McLeod had come back again with his stolen pack horses and was hanging around. *This must be him with that red hair. He has the chest of a giant gorilla. I don't like the smirk on his face or the fierce eyes.*

Liza didn't answer and tried to continue walking. She felt his bear-sized hand grip her arm and pull her back. "Let me go, sir. I must take the mail home!" she cried out. His grasp tightened, and she jumped with pain.

"Not so fast, my sweet. I haven't met you before, and I'm not in a hurry. I think you would smell pretty nice." He dropped the reins, and his horse stood still, blocking the narrow road. Red pulled her forward and began pushing his furry face into hers. Liza was repulsed by his filthy stench from days of no bathing. His grimy hand ripped at the front buttons of her dress while the other hand groped her skirt. Reeling with shock, Liza wriggled and pushed and tried to call out. It seemed hopeless. She wasn't strong enough to stop him. The iron grip of his hands was hurting. She screamed again and again.

In her terror, she didn't hear a horse come thundering up the road and the rider yelling, "Get off her!" Thomas catapulted from the horse onto the muscular shoulders of Red McLeod, pulling him backwards away from Liza's limp frame. Fists flew as Thomas smashed Red's face. Blood spurted from his nose and streaked his beard. Red roared with anger and struggled with Thomas, but he was taken by surprise and at a disadvantage. He pulled back, grabbed his hat, and threatened to get back at Thomas. He sputtered, "I'll find you another time, lassie," then leapt on his horse and charged back up the mountain trail.

Thomas pulled Liza to him and comforted her until she stopped quivering. "I've never been so afraid. What would he do to me?" she sobbed into his chest. It was too embarrassing to admit that Red's hands had been so hurtful. Then she realized that the front of her dress sagged open. Pulling the dress together, she struggled to fasten the buttons, while Thomas offered his jacket to cover her.

"I'll take you home on my horse. Don't worry I won't tell anybody. This can be our secret."

Winter 1917

~

Relationships between the four adults in the small house became closely intertwined. Each day, Wilbert and Thomas worked together, either building or clearing land to develop orchard space. Work could not begin on a new house until all the cleanup of the burnt one was done. Wilbert spent the winter months clearing the burnt house site. Finally, Wilbert proudly announced to Liza, "I found the carpenter, the one who built our last house. He has come back to Kaslo. He says he can make a similar house only bigger."

Liza, feeling exhausted from the cleanup work, brightened up and said, "Wilbert, that is such good news! Can we please have a bathing room and a toilet?"

Wilbert nodded emphatically. "Yes, I told him to include that in the plan. He says the building will take a couple years before we can move in. He will start as soon as the snow is gone in the spring."

"Well, I think I'll ask Mrs. Hanna to help me learn some of the Kootenai words so in the summer when the people from the south return with their canoes I might be able to talk with them," Liza said. "It'll help me pass the time." Wilbert nodded approval. He knew that the days were sometimes very tedious for Liza.

73

Rose became pregnant again and after several months of illness, had a miscarriage. She began to resent living on the flats, especially in the spring and summer with the insufferable mosquitoes. Even though Liza offered her some of the yarrow powder, she wouldn't try it because it made her skin look yellow. She gained weight and became surly, no longer the cheery woman who loved jokes and was good company for Liza. In spite of the Rose's gloominess, Liza was energetic and outgoing, eager to take on more work. She loved baking and cooking and especially providing favourites for the men, such as lacy sugar cookies.

Liza announced at breakfast one morning that because it was Friday it was a special baking day. "I'm planning to make wähe for dessert tonight. Should I make plum or apple?" Both Wilbert and Thomas looked up, excited at the thought of the traditional Swiss cake treat.

Wilbert said, "I want plum."

Thomas agreed, adding, "And lots of egg and cream topping!"

On the days that Liza did baking, the exotic cooking aromas drew Thomas's attention, and he spent more and more time hanging around the kitchen, waiting for a few private moments with Liza. One afternoon, when Wilbert left and Rose had taken Louise to get the mail, Thomas quietly came up behind Liza and put his hands on her slender waist. She backed away, startled. His fingers tightened more strongly, and then he pulled her toward him. The strength of his gaze commanded her to look at him. Liza was intimidated and yet excited. The voice inside her told her to pull away; she was almost paralyzed. Thomas, obviously aroused with her soft scent, managed to kiss her lips even as she pushed her face away.

"No, stop," Liza sputtered.

Thomas ignored the protestations and pulled her forward with one muscular arm. She struggled but was helpless. The scent of his sweat filled her nostrils. When she put her hands up to push him away, she felt the muscles of his chest. His virility was overwhelming, something she had never experienced. The more she pushed, the firmer his arm around her waist became, and he lifted her face with his hand and pressed his lips against hers. She knew this was wrong yet was more and more absorbed in his presence. The door banged, and they both jumped back, saved by the arrival. Liza gasped, "Wilbert is back!" *Could he have seen Thomas kissing me?*

With each passing day, Thomas found more frequent chances to corner Liza until finally he tricked her into helping him in the barn. In a hidden back corner, he coerced her again, and with his soft words and kisses she began to succumb until he managed to unbutton her dress and press his hand against her breast. Confused and stimulated, she let her body press into his hand, and he pulled her down into a mound of hay. Liza felt as if she were drifting on an untouchable cloud. The shy guilt began to dissolve as the ferocity of Thomas's kisses sent desire shooting through her body. And yet, an inner voice said, "Where is your loyalty to Wilbert?"

As the weeks went by, Liza tried to stay away from Thomas, until the next time she and Thomas were secretly together. When she was with Wilbert and Rose, she was sure her guilt was obvious to their eyes. The air in the house began to feel laden with secrets as the tension between Liza and Thomas increased.

She whispered to Thomas, "Do you think they know? I saw Rose glaring at me during dinner."

He shook his head. "Of course not."

Liza's emotions were more and more confused. She had always been taught to be loyal and truthful and to never betray her family. And now, with the long wait for her own house, she was bored and feeling

JUDY POLLARD

neglected by Wilbert because he was so preoccupied. Thomas seemed so romantic to her compared to Wilbert.

1918

~

Work on the new house kept Wilbert busy from dawn to dusk. The work was slow, and he felt frustrated, especially when he heard Thomas's frequent sarcastic questions about why the house was taking so long. Wilbert was too tired to give Liza attention, barely finishing his late dinner and falling into bed. Night after night he tossed, trying hard to sleep and ignore the dream pushing its way inside his brain, hearing Thomas's sarcastic voice and wondering whether he would ever stop being so obnoxious and self-righteous.

In his dreams of a beautiful new home, he sensed the licking of flames on the edges. His voice sounded frantic as he cried out for help, and he jolted himself awake. Liza sat up concerned and tried to calm him. "You're too tired from working so hard, and you can't sleep." Wilbert grunted agreement, and flopped over, trying to go back to sleep. He didn't want to talk about the dream.

One morning after breakfast, Liza pleaded with him. "Wilbert, when can I come and see the house? There must be something I can do."

Wilbert, looking thoughtful, remembered a conversation with the carpenter. "The carpenter will be away for a few days, so you could come tomorrow. The chimney is finished, and I will put a stove in the kitchen. You can help."

It was the first full day that Liza and Wilbert had spent together in months. As they struggled to place the stove correctly, Liza felt the enjoyment of working alongside Wilbert. Thinking about his calm, quiet temperament she realized the stress she'd been feeling at Thomas and Rose's house was easing. She thought about Wilbert's gentleness. *He doesn't say much, but he loves me. He's considerate . . . when we did sleep together, he wanted to please me, not hurt me . . . was I pushing him away? Is that why I have not gotten pregnant?*

Images of her responses to Thomas flooded Liza's mind. Conflicted, she turned to Wilbert and said, "I'm tired. I want to go outside and rest." She sat on a stump, her mind wracked by remorse. *How could I betray my faithful husband? He slaves away . . . do I deserve him? I must stop Thomas.*

Tears began trickling down her cheeks. She hadn't heard Wilbert's approach and was startled when he suddenly appeared, looking directly at her. Gently, he put his hands on her shoulders and asked, "What's wrong? You are crying?"

Embarrassed, Liza wiped her eyes. "I'm so tired of living with Thomas and Rose."

"I'm tired too. Rose always complains about the work. Thomas struts around like a peacock, trying to be in charge. Thinks he's something special, like when he was in the Swiss Guard years ago."

Liza nodded agreement. "I know what you mean. The only good part is baby Louise. But she's not our baby." Her tone had a hint of sadness.

"You really do want a baby of your own. I'm sorry I haven't been a good husband to you," Wilbert muttered. He pulled her to her feet and hugged her. "I promise to do better."

Liza was touched by his sincerity. *I must make Thomas stay away!*

But the frequency of Thomas's advances increased as he sensed that something had changed in Liza. He was sure he could control her as

THE DISTANCE

he had before, but she did not give in. Wilbert and Liza began to find private time for each other. Liza was able to encourage him, and within a couple of months she sensed that her body was changing. She was sure she was pregnant, finally! Her desire for a baby of her own was the daily mantra that dominated her emotions. She felt her heart was going into overdrive with excitement.

"Wilbert, I have news. I think I'm pregnant!"

He turned from reading. "You are? Finally? When do you think the baby will come?"

"In the spring. April, if I'm counting right. I need to go to the doctor in Kaslo to be sure," Liza responded nervously.

"Well, we will go to Kaslo," stated Wilbert. We can take the *Moyie*, stay overnight in a rooming house, and come back on the next trip."

"I'm glad you'll come with me. I'm shy about doctors."

The doctor confirmed the pregnancy and suggested that because of the long trip from Argenta to Kaslo, it was advisable for Liza to stay in a rooming house in Kaslo for some weeks prior to the delivery. Before leaving to go home, Liza and Wilbert made arrangements for her to stay in a rooming house for three weeks before the expected birthdate in the middle of April.

1919

~

After returning from their trip to the doctor in Kaslo, Liza and Wilbert talked about the details of all the things to be worked on in order to complete their new house during the winter. Fortunately, the winter was mild and spring arrived early. Liza busied herself with arranging the kitchen and making curtains.

Finally, all was ready and they moved in, exhausted and relieved to be in their home to welcome their baby. The spring brought the return of robins, sparrows, and chickadees, flitting from branch to branch and filling the air with songs. A burst of new life!

It was a sparkling morning as Liza slowly walked down the path to the wharf, absorbing the scents in the air. As she came to the edge of the steep drop down the hillside, she stopped to admire the breadth of the flats stretched out to the north of the lake. A carpet of yellow-green early leaves from the dense cottonwood trees spread gently over the flats, filling the air with a sweet perfume that she found almost intoxicating. It was so intense that she decided to sit and rest before continuing.

Later that morning, when she went home with the mail, Liza told Wilbert about the spring return of the Kootenai people. "Wilbert, Malyan was at the wharf today. She came to see me and rub my big belly. So friendly. We laughed together, and I tickled her little one." Liza giggled and gave Wilbert a hug.

Wilbert smiled. "I'm surprised that you two seem to be so friendly, even though you can't say much to each other."

"I'm still trying to learn more words from Mrs. Hanna, but it takes me a long time because I don't see her often. Maybe when the baby comes, she will visit more."

The next week Liza took the *Moyie* to Kaslo and moved into the rooming house. Baby Jessie arrived a week earlier than predicted, so it was a good thing that Liza was already in Kaslo and could be quickly taken to the Queen Victoria Hospital. A telegraph message was sent to Argenta to tell Wilbert of the birth of his daughter. Liza was surprised when he arrived a day later.

"You came so soon. Isn't she beautiful?" questioned Liza as she held the baby out to Wilbert. "Her perfect head smells like fresh apples."

Astonished at the thought of holding the sleeping infant, Wilbert pulled back. "Umm, yes, she is. I don't know how to hold her," he mumbled apprehensively.

Liza called to the nurse, "Please show my husband how to hold the baby." She reassured Wilbert, "The nurses here are wonderful. They are trained and are part of the Victorian Order of Nurses. We can trust them."

After some tentative efforts, Wilbert finally held Jessie close to his chest and stared with disbelief at the perfection of her tiny nose placed exactly in the centre of her round face, her pink cheeks and lips, dark hair like Liza's, and even a double chin. For a brief moment, Jessie woke up and gazed at him with wide-set blue eyes. He felt as if he had been given a gift of love.

THE DISTANCE

Liza and Jessie stayed in the hospital for another week before Wilbert came back and escorted them home on the *Moyie*. He helped them into the wagon for the bumpy ride up the mountainside to the house. Liza hesitantly entered as if she didn't really know the place; it was still so new and unfamiliar.

Wilbert insisted that they go immediately to the bedroom. "You must see," he said firmly to Liza. In the bedroom, there was a small wooden cradle! It was supported by a stand at each end so it could be rocked, and it was lined with a colourful woven blanket sent from Switzerland by Liza's mother.

"Wilbert, you made this?" Liza exclaimed joyously. "And you painted the animals on the side?" She gently wrapped the sleeping Jessie in a soft blanket and placed her in the cradle, then turned to hug Wilbert. "Thank you, thank you, thank you!"

Liza adjusted quickly to caring for a tiny baby. She was soon able to take advantage of Jessie's naps and use the time to start baking again— after she'd finished scrubbing diapers. One thing she didn't manage was to work in the vegetable garden. "Wilbert I'm worried about the garden. It needs attention now so we'll have vegetables for the summer and fall. I tried wrapping Jessie in the baby wrap I've seen others use, but when I bend over it squeezes her, and she gets cranky. On nice days I could take her outside in some sort of bed."

Wilbert replied, "I remember at home the mothers had prams to put babies in and take them out of the house. But we don't have one, and besides, it wouldn't work here on the uneven ground. Maybe I could find a box and put a soft lining in it so you could use it outside."

"I think that might work," said Liza. "Let's try it."

A box was found, and Liza tried it in the garden, moving it around to be close to her so she could hear Jessie and talk to her. But then bug season started. "The bugs are back in force," complained Liza. "They love chewing Jessie's tender skin! I won't be to have Jessie outside until late summer. The weeds are taking over the tiny shoots of plants. It's so frustrating!"

Wilbert thoughtfully took a puff on his pipe. "Hmm, maybe I could try to look after Jessie tomorrow morning to give you more time in the garden," he said. "But I'm not sure I can change a diaper without sticking the pin into her too."

"That's a wonderful idea!" Liza exclaimed. "I'll feed her right after breakfast and put her in bed for a nap, then I'll go straight to work in the garden. In the meantime, I'll give you a lesson on changing diapers. You haven't really tried it out."

The plan seemed to be working, and Liza, assisted by her fat chickens consuming bugs between the rows, had almost finished the large weeding task when she heard shrieks from the house. She ran in to find Wilbert standing over Jessie, looking aghast at her beet red tiny face that was emitting furious howls. "What happened?" asked Liza as she noticed the unfastened diaper under Jessie.

"I poked her with the diaper pin," Wilbert mumbled, almost in tears. "She wiggles so much, and I was trying to be careful."

Liza checked to see where the pin had poked Jessie and saw only a minor scratch. She picked Jessie up to calm her and explained to Wilbert that no real harm had been done even though both Jessie and Wilbert were traumatized. "I didn't know it was so complicated to do simple things with babies," he moaned.

"Yes, it does take practice. I hope you'll keep trying. Jessie and I need your help."

Liza suggested that Wilbert hold Jessie, look into her eyes, and talk to her so she'd get used to him. To Wilbert's surprise, when he did so,

THE DISTANCE

Jessie focused her strong gaze on his eyes. Soon Jessie started gurgling in response to Wilbert's utterances. "Liza she's talking back to me, just like she does to you!" he said with delight. Liza secretly rejoiced inside to hear Wilbert's enthusiasm. She knew he had a hard time having a baby in their lives. *He's not a talkative person and babies need to have their parents talk to them and show them they care . . . he's trying.*

Jessie attracted the attention of helpful neighbours coming to admire her delicate features and assure Liza about her healthy growth. Mrs. Filipek exclaimed her amazement when Liza told her that Jessie rarely woke up at night, even when only a few months old. Rose brought Louise to meet the new baby and promised they would return often. Thomas was busy at work, which secretly pleased Liza because she didn't want to see him.

On Liza's birthday, Wilbert had a surprise. After breakfast, he told Liza to sit in her favourite chair because he had something for her. He went to the barn and returned carrying something large. Liza was mystified and said, "What is that?"

Wilbert gave her a hug and put the bulky gift in her arms. "It's a cradle pack like the one you admired. I understand it is the custom of some people that a new pack be created for a new baby. I do admit it took me a long time to make."

Liza, astonished and teary, exclaimed, "I can't believe you would make this for me. It's so much work, and you have so much to do already. How did you ever find the time? How did you know how to make it?"

Wilbert explained that he had seen Kootenai people at the wharf with cradle packs and looked discreetly to see how they were put together. He had been secretly working on the project in the barn for a couple months. As she lifted the cradle pack and examined the detail, she could tell it was very similar to the one she saw on Malyan's back. She slipped it on. "It fits. When Jessie wakes up, we can try her in it." Liza jumped up and gave Wilbert a huge hug. Wilbert felt thrilled. He often thought he didn't know how to be a good enough husband and how to please Liza. *I'm glad she's so happy . . . maybe I'm learning . . .*

By late July, the garden was producing fresh vegetables. It was Liza's favourite place, working with young plants and finding the first peas and beans to cook for dinner. The morning summer air was warm and would become hot by midday, so Liza took baby Jessie in her cradle pack, singing softly to her as she knelt between rows of vegetables. Wilbert called to her from the barn that he was leaving with the horse and wagon.

Just as Liza turned to talk to him, she noticed someone leading a tall grey horse as he strode along the path from Vadas's place. Liza watched him with increasing apprehension, realizing that he looked familiar. *No, not him! I would know that red hair and filthy beard anywhere! It must be Red McLeod!*

She jumped to her feet, jolting Jessie so that she awoke and yelled, "Wilbert, don't leave! Come here." She could feel her heartbeat quicken.

Wilbert with a puzzled expression looked around. "Why?" he called out. As he turned his head, he saw the large man striding nonchalantly like a bull elk toward the garden where Liza and Jessie were.

"I wonder if that's Red McLeod," Wilbert muttered to Liza as he stood beside her. Liza, her eyes agape, stiffened with fear.

"Hello, I haven't met you before," the man said boldly to Wilbert. "I'm Red McLeod, known in these parts." He stood tall over both Wilbert and Liza, looking down at them with disdain. "What's this I see? This lassie and with a babe now."

Liza stepped closer to Wilbert, seeking protection from Red's intense glare. Her mind was swarmed by the ugly memory of that stench in her face and the filthy hands on her body. She wanted to hide behind Wilbert.

THE DISTANCE

Red McLeod grunted threateningly. "That's not the guy that came along when I was making friends with you. I've been looking for him to bloody his face!"

Wilbert, confused and worried, looked at Liza, and then at McLeod, before he growled, "What do you want here? You better be on your way before I get my rifle."

McLeod, with a sardonic look, pulled the rein of his horse and began moving slowly past the garden. "I can always come back," he taunted over his shoulder.

Liza, now shaking with panic, collapsed. She sobbed, "That is Red McLeod. I would never forget him. He's such a vile man."

Wilbert stood looking down at her, his face contorted with suspicion. "You've met him before?"

Liza nodded and explained how she had been attacked by Red McLeod a couple years earlier.

"What did he mean, about the guy whose face he wants to bloody?" demanded Wilbert.

Liza avoided Wilbert's eyes as she choked out, "Thomas. Thomas came just in time and saved me."

"Why didn't you tell me?" questioned Wilbert.

"I was too scared to talk about it. He attacked me. I was ashamed," said Liza hesitantly. She burst into tears, and Jessie, still in the cradle pack, wailed along with her mother.

"You should have told me. I'm supposed to protect you," Wilbert said as he stomped toward the barn. The turmoil in his head was almost blinding. *She hid this from me. Thomas was there, of course—happy to save her.* Wilbert's sense of contentment with the new house and baby began to be eroded by the old resentments toward Thomas, the resentments that forever simmered, waiting for the fire to get hotter. Memories of

87

Thomas's superior attitude, his manipulation, and his self-righteousness seethed inside Wilbert. He doubted that Thomas even remembered that his stubbornness was responsible for Hubert's death in the river.

As the weeks of summer and early fall passed by, Liza was grateful for the abundance of the garden and wild huckleberries and busied herself making preserves for the winter. Wilbert had never said another word about Red McLeod, to her relief. She had heard from Mrs. Hanna that Red McLeod had left for the winter, returning to the Fort Steele area and staying out of the way of the Northwest Mounted Police. *I never want to see that man again,* she thought.

Early Fall 1919

~

Wilbert and Filipek were up the mountain preparing the water pipeline for the upcoming winter. Suddenly they were threatened by a snarling black bear. Filipek grabbed his rifle and muttered, "Same bear that's been hanging around our house. No more chances for him." He took a quick aim and fired. As they stood over the inert black mass, the two men agreed to skin and butcher the bear and divide the meat. Filipek would take the front quarters and a hind quarter, while Wilbert would take the other hind quarter. Wilbert was unsure what Liza would think about that but remembered that Mrs. Hanna had offered to help Liza can bear meat in her pressure cooker if there was meat available. So, he agreed to take the meat after the butchering.

A few days later, Mrs. Hanna brought her pressure cooker to Liza's kitchen, where they sliced the meat into chunks, carefully extracting the wormiest parts, then packed it tightly into glass sealing jars. Rubber rings were positioned carefully on the top edges of the jars, and then a glass lid was set on top, which was held tightly in place with a screwed-on metal ring. A vibrant fire heated Liza's stovetop where the large heavy metal cooker sat full of water, and soon it was the perfect temperature for several jars to be placed on the basket inside. The thick metal lid of the cooker was fastened to the pot with sturdy clamps. A temperature

89

gauge poked out on the top of the lid to allow regulation of the water temperature inside.

As the filled pot gained heat, steam hissed from the small valve which bobbed up and down beside the temperature gauge. Mrs. Hanna explained that it all needed careful monitoring during the process. After an hour of the water boiling and the temperature remaining consistent, the pot was taken off the stove to cool for half an hour. Fortunately, the large handles protruding from each side made lifting the heavy pot possible without getting burned.

Mrs. Hanna looked at the temperature and stated, "I think it's safe now. I'll show you how to open the clamps and take the pot lid off."

Liza nervously followed Mrs. Hanna's directions, and soon the jars were out of the pot and placed on a wooden board. After each jar cooled, the tightness of the seal between the glass lid and the rubber ring was checked to be sure the meat would be fully processed and safe to store so they could eat it in the winter.

"Well, that's a job well done. Let's have some tea and cake now," said Mrs. Hanna approvingly. Liza nodded agreement, glad to have more food for the winter.

Both Liza and Wilbert enjoyed their warm bed in the winter chill, and by mid-winter, Liza knew another baby was on the way. Even though she was surprised because Jessie was not yet a year old, both she and Wilbert looked forward to being a family of four. Wilbert was sure the baby would be a boy this time.

After years of living in the valley bottom at Thomas and Rose's place on the flats, it was surprising how different the snow felt at the new house during the winter. The snow on the flats was wet, often crisscrossed by channels of running water, barely covered by a thin layer of ice. Busy ducks scrambled over each other for open water and juicy tidbits.

THE DISTANCE

Higher up, with the thermometer reading zero or colder, it snowed and snowed. During storms, the wind whistled and howled, creating banked snowdrifts around the buildings. Shovelling through packed snow to make pathways to the barn was arduous work.

Wood had to be chopped and carried into the porch every day, and the fires stoked all night to keep the house warm. Wilbert bought a wood heater in Kaslo and put it into the hallway so that the central part of the house had heat. Jessie's little bed was moved closer to the heater to keep her warm. In between the storms, the sky cleared and brilliant sun sparkled off every surface. Pristine snow billowed around the edges of the roofs, appearing like a painting of a magical dance of feathers and gauze.

"Wilbert, have you looked out the window? This snow reminds me of home in Switzerland. The peaks of the mountains across the valley are like knife blades against the pure blue sky." Liza heard snores in response and looked at Wilbert, who was having a nap before trudging out for another load of wood. She was grateful to have him doing the work. *It's a good thing he's here. I'm too tired after caring for Jessie and cooking and cleaning and laundry. I'll be glad to see spring. Who will look after Jessie when I go to Kaslo in the summer for the new baby?*

1920

~

Liza's worries about who would stay with Jessie when she gave birth to the new baby were settled when she learned that Wilbert's sister was coming in June. Before her arrival, Liza cleaned the small house meticulously and placed bunches of pine needles in the rooms to freshen the air. Maria arrived from Switzerland excited to visit and eager to help Liza with all her responsibilities. She had grown children, so she was experienced as a parent and delighted to instruct Liza about the best way to do almost everything. Jessie was walking and running, and then soon after, was climbing and falling, with Maria to the rescue. Liza knew Jessie would be in good hands when she went to Kaslo.

The new baby was a boy. When Wilbert got the telegram that the baby was born, he was so excited that he borrowed a rowboat and rowed to Kaslo the very next day. He burst into the hospital to Liza's surprise and greeted her with a huge hug—quite out of character for him!

"Wilbert, how did you get here?"

"I borrowed Steve's rowboat. It only took three hours with the lake being so calm."

Liza, amazed at his eagerness, said, "Wonderful! I'm impressed."

"I had to see my son," he said. "I know what to call him: Peter, or Pete for short. Like my favourite uncle."

"Oh, I wanted to ask if you had a name," Liza said. "I like Peter." So the name was settled. Several days later, Liza and Pete travelled home to Argenta on the *Moyie* as Wilbert had taken the rowboat and returned earlier. When Liza, carrying a bundled-up Pete, emerged from the boat, she was thrilled to see Wilbert, Jessie, and Maria, accompanied by several other friends and neighbours. Liza was congratulated with many hugs. Pete was admired by everyone, although he slept through the adoration. It was a special event to have a newborn baby join the community.

Baby Pete replaced Jessie in the cradle, and Jessie graduated to a small crib bed, made especially for her during the winter by Wilbert. All the rooms in the house were full and busy. Maria was invaluable with the housework and caring for Jessie, while Liza spent most of her time with Pete.

"Maria, I'm so grateful to have you here helping. It's been six months already since you came," said Liza.

"Yes, it has," replied Maria, "and I will need to be returning home very soon. My father has become ill, and I'm needed there."

"I wondered how your parents were because Wilbert mentioned he had a letter from his sister Millie recently and she said there was some illness," Liza said. "I completely understand your need to return, although we will greatly miss you here."

"And I will miss you. I will always remember the joy of seeing Jessie become a lively little girl and Pete developing baby charms. I expect I will leave within two weeks, as soon as I can find the tickets I need to travel."

At dinner that evening, Maria and Liza shared their conversation with Wilbert. He also expressed his gratitude for her help and offered to make arrangements for her by sending telegrams and booking travel tickets. The plans were made quickly.

Both Liza and Wilbert were sad about Maria's upcoming departure. She was so easy to take into their family. "It has made such a difference to have Maria here all that time hasn't it, Wilbert? She helps with everything yet doesn't interfere with us learning to be parents to two children," commented Liza.

Wilbert noticed tears dripping down Liza's cheeks as he replied, "She has made our lives much easier. I think she's helped us have a good start for our bigger family." Liza nodded agreement and wiped her tears.

Then she suggested, "Perhaps before Maria leaves we could invite Thomas and Rose and Louise to come for dinner. It's been a long time since we had dinner together because life has been so busy with the new house and the babies."

"Ya, we could do that," responded Wilbert.

Maria and Liza planned an elaborate dinner with Swiss specialties that they knew would please people. When the guests arrived, Wilbert and Thomas stayed outside talking business until the table was ready. Rose seemed tired and quiet. She commented, "It would have been nice if Maria had time to help me before going home." Both Liza and Maria were taken aback by the comment as she had not expressed this thought earlier in Maria's visit.

"I'm sure I'll return," said Maria, "and I hope to stay with you next time."

During the dinner conversation, Rose mentioned to Thomas that Maria said she would come again and stay with them next time. Thomas responded with a slight scowl, "I guess Wilbert and Liza are tired of having somebody else in the house." Rose was startled by his response.

95

Liza jumped in and quickly spoke, "Not at all. She has helped us so much. Wilbert thinks so too."

Wilbert abruptly stood up and left the table to get another plate of food. He loudly muttered, "Thomas, being as obnoxious as usual."

The evening ended early as the children needed to go to bed. There was a sense of regret that the conversation hadn't been more good-natured. Maria left the following week and journeyed home.

Spring 1921

~

*W*inter had been short. The weather was dry and sunny, and the snow was melting quickly, leaving large patches of dirt and mud even in the shady places. Wilbert and Thomas agreed to start clearing trees in higher areas on the mountain early this year because the wagon trails were passable. They wanted to begin opening more area for orchards.

It was early morning; the sun hadn't yet poked its way over the peaks of Mount Willet. Wilbert stepped out the kitchen door and gazed at the view of the distant mountain ridge already basking in the sunlight. Circling overhead was an osprey that had returned from its winter trip south. It seemed to have something in its beak. A loud shriek pierced the air, and a bald eagle dived at the osprey. Pushing it aside, the eagle snatched the food, before spreading its broad wings and flying back to the perch at the top of the nearby fir tree, screeching victoriously. Wilbert watched. He imagined there could be a smug look in the eagle's intense eyes, and he dreaded that this might be a foretelling of the coming day with Thomas.

Inside the barn, the mountain air had the damp chill of a new day. Wilbert had already fed the two Belgian draught horses and gotten out the harnesses for the wagon by the time Thomas arrived, puffing after his hike up the hill from his house.

As he led the horses out of the barn, Wilbert muttered to Thomas, "These horses don't want to cooperate. Not much snow left, but they're stubborn. The harnesses are cold and stiff, and I need to get the wagon hooked up. Can you give me a hand?"

Thomas pushed impatiently on the flank of Bessie. "Never did like this one much. Stubborn like my wife."

Wilbert looked up in surprise. "What?"

"Nothing." Thomas stomped around to the other side of the horse, avoiding Wilbert.

The two horses crowded together in the chill, rustling the half-frozen snow with their feet. Thomas pushed between them, brushing dirt from their legs and cleaning caked mud and snow from the large, hairy hooves. Both horses tolerated the attention and bent their heads to watch, snorting warm breath down his back. Thomas had to elbow the two of them in the ribs to get breathing room. "Get over there!" he grumbled. Just at that moment, Bessie turned to bite Bert's neck, causing him to jump sideways and pull hard on the halter rope.

Wilbert whacked the gelding with an open hand on the shoulder, "Stop that!" A ton of muscles clenched in response, eyes suddenly alert. "That'll make them pay attention!" exclaimed Wilbert. "Let's finish getting the harness on these two." He rubbed Bert's nose and whispered in his ear, "I know how you feel. That bully won't let you alone. I should call her Thomas!"

Thomas fastened the harness, almost begrudgingly. Wilbert noticed and thought, *Thomas is annoyed, again . . . I'll mind my own business.*

The wagon trail led through an open slope that had already been logged, so the ground was exposed to the warming sun. The air was filled with the dank heaviness of the soil surface, releasing weeks of frost and snow and opening to welcome warmth. Many of the stumps had been blown up with dynamite, and the lumpy ground was ready to be smoothed and prepared for planting seedling fruit trees. They entered the darkness of the thick fir and cedar, where the forest floor was scattered with patches of semi-frozen snow in between the layers of decaying, yellowish-brown vegetation left from the fall. Shrubs, not much more than skinny sticks, were still waiting for sap to enliven the branches.

The path then led past Hubert's grave, marked by the wooden cross. Wilbert's mind was jolted with a flashback of Hubert's shrieks and his flailing hand in the water, rising and falling. The intensity of the memory brought tears to his eyes.

"Let's stop and check Hubert's grave. I haven't been here for ages," suggested Wilbert. "I can't put the memory of his drowning out of my mind."

"What's the point? I never go back to graves. Let the brush take care of it," was Thomas's curt response.

Wilbert was shocked at Thomas's lack of feeling for Hubert. *I always knew he couldn't care less about Hubert and what happened.*

Urging the horses forward past the gravesite, Thomas insisted on taking a shortcut, despite Wilbert's objections that there would be trouble because of the icy and muddy parts on the narrow trail. There was also a steep edge that looked especially slick.

"Slow down, Thomas. There's barely enough room for the horses on this section, and the outside edge is ice."

Thomas scoffed at Wilbert's caution and continued to move the horses forward. With a jolt, Bert, on the outside of the trail, slid to the right, his front hoof catching on a boulder just over the edge. Bessie jerked, and the wagon lurched to a stop.

JUDY POLLARD

"I told you there would be a problem," muttered Wilbert as he leapt off the seat and tried to calm Bert.

Thomas jumped down, ran to the front of the team, and pulled on the harness, trying to steady the team of horses.

Wilbert glared at Thomas as he began to unhitch the harness so that he could lead Bert forward and up onto the trail. He cursed, "Damn. Look at this. Bert has thrown a shoe. Now we'll have to get back somehow and replace it. Naturally, that job has to be done by me, since you don't know how." After carefully checking Bert to be sure there weren't other injuries, Wilbert began to lead him around the wagon and back to the trail.

Thomas yelled, "So you're gonna leave me here with only one horse?"

"Ya, well, you caused the problem in the first place." Wilbert felt the stirring of his ever-present annoyance as the heat rose inside his chest and irritated his throat. He had nothing more to say before tromping down the trail.

When he arrived at the shed, Wilbert secured Bert to a post and built a hot blaze in the forge, ready to prepare a horseshoe and replace the damaged one. He impatiently held the shoe over the fire to heat it, talking to himself. "He'll never smarten up. He struts around, likes to be lord and master . . . everybody thinks he's the one that gets things done, ha!"

Once the shoe was glowing red hot, Wilbert held it in place and smashed the metal with the hammer in his other hand. Clang! Clang! Each strike was louder than the last. The flame tongues felt as if they were searing the inside of his chest. Finally the horseshoe was shaped, and he set it in the bucket of icy water to quench and cool it enough to set on the hoof. Steam hissed from the surface of the water while Wilbert stomped around the shed telling himself to calm down so he

100

THE DISTANCE

wouldn't transfer his angst to Bert when he cleaned the hoof and nailed the new shoe in place.

By the time Thomas returned with Bessie and the wagon, Wilbert had replaced Bert's shoe and pronounced him ready for work the next day. The air of tension was so evident that Liza noticed and at dinner asked Wilbert if he was upset. He grunted, "Just Thomas and his bull-headedness again."

In the pre-dawn light the next morning, Wilbert stirred himself awake from a dream-filled sleep. High-pitched howls echoed through the trees as the coyotes told each other where the tastiest prey was located. *Probably the chicken coop,* he thought hazily. There was heaviness in the back of his head and a deep voice with derisive tones; he sensed the voice change to soft seduction, and there was a whiff of perfume—Liza's?

He sat up in bed, shaking his head, telling himself to wake up and check the chicken coop. The old dream had returned, even more annoying after Thomas's disregard for Hubert's grave and the dispute about Bert and Bessie. He felt the familiar resentment invade his body, knowing he had to tolerate another day of working with Thomas.

Summer 1921

~

The mail brought letters from home, including one from Maria. The letter told of worry about Rose, who had written to say that she wasn't feeling well and that Thomas was angry most of the time. Maria wrote of her surprise with the news that Rose and Thomas were moving from their beautiful house on the flats to the old hotel building at the wharf.

Although Liza knew that Rose and Thomas had already moved to a different house, she was alarmed at Maria's comments, and questioned Wilbert. "Wilbert, how is Thomas when you're working together?"

"Bossy as usual. Nothing ever pleases him. There's nothing that can be done. It's the way he is." Wilbert obviously didn't want to talk about it.

"You told me that there is a chance to acquire more land because the government is encouraging fruit growing. I thought you and Thomas already made an agreement."

"Ya, before we moved here. Now we might be able to get a better deal. I'm going on a trip to Nelson to meet with the government agent. I'll be gone for a few days."

"Is Thomas going also?"

"No. I'm going alone. Don't trust him so much anymore. I can negotiate better than he can."

"I'll get your things ready for you. I think while you're gone, I'll visit Rose and see if I can cheer her up. That seems like a neighbourly thing to do. Maria seems pretty worried about her."

After Wilbert left, Liza put Jessie and Pete in the wagon and set off down the trail. As she approached the house, she could hear Thomas's angry voice. "You're lazy. Can't you even cook a good dinner?" Rose burst out the door and crashed into Liza, who wasn't sure what she was hearing and seeing. She made a quick decision that maybe the best help she could give would be to take Rose away from Thomas.

"Rose, would you like to come to my house, and we could do some gardening together? My beans are ready to pick."

Rose tearfully looked at Liza and nodded. "Thanks. Yes, I want to come. Let's go." The two women took all of the children up the trail to the Jeannerets' house, Liza trying to chat along the way to relieve Rose's obvious distress. As the women worked together, Rose became involved in the work and seemed grateful to have green beans and lettuce to take home.

The summer weather was hot and dry, perfect for ripening the raspberries in Liza's garden. With both children settled in their beds for an afternoon nap, Liza hummed to herself as she carefully plucked the plump berries off the branches. She wanted them to be perfectly shaped in preparation for preserving. A rustle of the bush behind her alerted her, and she turned to find Thomas staring down at her. She could smell liquor on his breath.

"What are you doing, Thomas?"

"Just here to look after you. Wilbert didn't want me to go, so I guess my job is to look after you. Like I've done before. Remember Red McLeod?"

"That was a long time ago. You smell bad. You should leave."

THE DISTANCE

Thomas leaned over and cradled her waist with his broad hands. "Maybe I've had a few drinks, but I don't smell nearly as bad as Red."

Liza pulled back as hard as she could, trapped on two sides by the thick, prickly raspberry bushes. "You're making me scared. I'm going to scream."

"Won't do you any good. Nobody here. I remember when you were living with me and Rose, and you were pretty friendly. Seemed like you wanted me around then."

Liza, like a caged ferret, clawed at his face, but he grabbed her hands, pulled her forward, and began kissing her neck and chest. She felt herself being pushed underneath his heavy body and her head hitting the ground with force. She knew his power was more than she could fend off, and she was afraid if he injured her, nobody would be there to look after Jessie and Pete. She closed her mind and her eyes.

When she dared to look, she saw him standing over her prone body and could feel the dishevelled skirt and torn buttons. "You should get yourself cleaned up. Don't worry, Wilbert will never find out."

Liza, alone, terrified, and confused, vowed to herself that nobody would ever know. She would force it out of her mind. Six weeks later she began to wonder whether it was possible to keep it out of her mind. Another baby was on the way.

Spring 1922

~

The winter had been long, with many severe snowstorms and cold days. Just keeping the fires stoked and the house warm for the family kept Liza very busy and exhausted as the due date came closer. She wished for warm winds and soft rain. *I wouldn't be so tired then*, she thought. Because the fierce weather continued, she suggested to Wilbert that she go into Kaslo a week before the expected date to be sure she wouldn't be trapped by bad weather. She knew that they needed to plan for the care of Jessie and Pete while she was away, so she suggested to Wilbert, "Do you think Gertrude and Millie would come to help out for a while?"

Wilbert wrote immediately to his sisters and asked them to come, offering to make the arrangements for them. They were delighted and quickly confirmed that they would start packing. They arrived just in time, in the midst of the unrelenting March storms.

Liza had always been struck by the similarities between Gertrude and Millie, even though they were six years apart in age. They were short in stature, like Wilbert, and unlike Rose, who was taller and more robust. Both had thick dark hair pulled back severely from the face, wide-set blue eyes, and even noses, mouths, and chins. Their soft complexions were smooth, and they looked well-nourished. An air of calm self-assurance emanated from their friendly eyes.

Gertrude, being older, was quick to take charge of situations, and Millie was a cooperative assistant to her. Every day, they visited Liza and were wonderful aunties to the children, taking some of the work off her shoulders. In the fall, they would be returning to Switzerland.

Liza was relieved to be safely in Kaslo in time for the birth of the baby, who they named Daniel. He was a big baby, more than nine pounds, where the others had been closer to seven pounds. His little body had a solid roundness to it, with skin folds in his arms and thighs. Long, dark hair framed his face with his half-closed eyes and pink chubby cheeks.

Liza and Wilbert arrived home with Daniel to an excited greeting party. Gertrude, Millie, and the children had made a special cake and decorated the house with early-blooming wildflowers—white daisies and bright yellow dandelions. Jessie and Pete crowded around Liza, more interested in the baby than their mother. Daniel slept peacefully despite the flood of adoration and the tentative holding of his tiny body as he was passed from person to person.

"It's amazing he can sleep through all this," commented Millie.

Liza agreed, "He's such a sleeper! All he seems to need is milk and sleep. I'm glad he doesn't mind the commotion around him. I wondered what it would be like when we got home with Jessie and Pete adding their noise and action to his surroundings."

Jessie proudly proclaimed to Liza that she had prepared the baby crib for Daniel and led her into the bedroom to show off the crib, complete with carefully folded blankets. Liza hugged her. "Thank you. I'm so proud of all the things you can do, and I know you'll be a big help with Daniel, and of course Pete too."

THE DISTANCE

"Yes, I will. Aunt Gertrude taught me how to fold the blankets," Jessie proclaimed.

The house was full with the family of five plus Gertrude and Millie, who were invaluable help in accomplishing all the work. Recognizing that the house was too crowded, Gertrude and Millie decided to move to Thomas and Rose's place because there was extra room there. They still climbed the hill every morning to help Liza and Wilbert with the busy family. Millie had learned to enjoy milking the cow and making butter, so that took one of Liza's responsibilities off her shoulders.

The hot days of summer arrived and, as often as possible, Gertrude and Millie hiked down the hill to the beach on the lake so Jessie and Pete could have a swim. Liza was thankful to have the house to herself and Daniel. It gave her some time to garden and time to rest when Daniel slept. Daniel put on weight rapidly and was soon rolling over and then sitting up, to the cheers of Jessie and Pete. They never lost their fascination with their baby brother.

Late August 1922

~

Since spring, the weather had been hot with little rain. Thankfully the mosquito infestation had been short-lived; however, the woods were dangerously dried out, and everyone was aware that it would take just the slightest spark to start a dangerous forest fire.

Wilbert bounced comfortably on the wagon seat as Bessie and Bert trudged up the steep mountain trail. He was looking forward to another day working on his own, without Thomas. A thunderstorm during the night had passed quickly after refreshing the heavy, dusty air. That morning, Wilbert was enveloped by the musky aroma of the forest that crowded the edges of the road. Breathing deeply, he filled his lungs with the soothing fragrance. He had no memory of breathing such strengthening air when he lived in Switzerland. He knew the decision thirteen years ago to move to the wilds of Canada had been the right one to make.

It would be another day of hard labour as Wilbert was going to the marked property line to fall more trees and clean brush to make a clear boundary that would be far above the clearing of their house. The project of encircling the one hundred and twenty acres of land would take years to complete. Rather than feeling discouraged, Wilbert felt a sense of pride as he could now see some results of his backbreaking labour materializing in the form of a line stretching up the mountainside and visible from the lakeshore. The image of his work on the slopes was comforting.

It was more than a year now since the new house on the mountainside was complete, and Wilbert and Liza and the children had settled into it. Wilbert could almost feel his heart clenching when he remembered the agonies of the past years. He could hear the voice repeating inside: . . . *fire was devastating, we were trapped into living with Thomas and Rose. If only I could be a better husband . . . what I know about is work. She's happier in the new house.*

He took another deep breath. The doubts assaulting his mind would pass. *It'll be alright.* Wilbert began to relax as he rode along and soaked in the warm sun. He could see the clearing with their house and barn when he looked down the mountain toward the lake, and he could hear the occasional shrieks of Pete and Jessie chasing each other.

Suddenly he smelled smoke in the air. He cautiously looked from side to side, his eyes finally spotting a small flicker in the tinder-dry undergrowth. Sure enough, there was a tiny wisp of smoke. He jumped from the wagon and ran to it. By the time he got there, a flame was leaping toward a nearby pile of debris. It lapped onto the next pile, and Wilbert, adrenalin pumping, ran for a shovel to dump soil on the flames. His efforts were soon undone by the flames, and he became frantic.

His heart was in his throat. He leapt into the wagon and whipped the horses to race down the mountain. He needed help and water. Most of the neighbours lived far away. By the time he found Thomas and Mr. Hanna and they returned with him, the flames were arcing up the dry bark of several trees. The men decided to clear a break in the hope that the fire would be held back between it and the nearby Argenta Creek. They worked frantically, chopping and hauling brush. Thomas raced

THE DISTANCE

from the creek with bucket after bucket of water, sweat dripping into his eyes, shoulder muscles bulging from the strain. From his previous experience in fighting a forest fire on the flats, Thomas had learned to notice potential hotspots and hollered at Hanna and Wilbert, pointing to places to dump water.

Feeling almost on the point of collapse, Wilbert stopped for breath and leaned on his shovel. Thomas came up behind him with a sarcastic remark, "What were you doing? Daydreaming as usual? You should have noticed earlier that something was wrong."

Wilbert kept his back to Thomas and refused to look at him. "How do you know what was happening? Just be helpful," he barked.

Thomas, at Wilbert's side, continued to egg him on, insinuating that if Wilbert had been quicker, the fire wouldn't have spread. Wilbert was fed up; his fury ignited by Thomas's tone and physical superiority. He had hoped that by moving into the new house and away from Thomas, the frequent turmoil he felt would drift away. But now it was all back.

Wilbert and Hanna dug a wide trench around the perimeter of the flames, while Thomas continued to haul buckets. Exhaustion had begun to set in, but they didn't take time to sit. Once in a while, each man went to the creek, splashed icy water over his head, and gulped a welcome swallow of water. Finally, the flames died down.

After several hours, they decided the fire guard would be effective and agreed to take turns staying on watch. Hanna said he would ask his two sons to take turns as well. They all knew the fire could erupt again at any time over the next days. That was a close call! Much could have been lost with the fire coming so close to Wilbert and Liza's new home. The memory of their first home burning down was still alarming for both of them.

Wilbert went home to a welcome dinner before he fell into bed. The night air was close and humid, causing him to toss around in spite of exhausted muscles that craved relaxation. When he was able to sleep, ghosts returned to his turbulent mind: screams from Hubert as he flailed in the river years ago; menacing insults from Thomas always trying to dominate; a glimpse of Liza pulling back from Thomas's hands; fires burning; eagles intensely watching and waiting. Sleeping was almost worse than having to work with Thomas during the day.

*

I SHOOK MY HEAD. "I can't imagine having so many torments in your mind. Wilbert tenaciously kept trying to get away from them, but after things seemed to settle down, another one would emerge. I don't know if I could keep from exploding."

Hans nodded agreement. "It almost seems like he was starting to go crazy with demons chasing each other in his mind. Did Liza know how disturbed he was getting, I wonder?"

"There was always so much work to do every day that Wilbert had to focus on the demands and couldn't just be consumed with his fears. One thing he prided himself on was that he was an exceptionally hard worker and accomplished a lot every day. He didn't complain to others much." I replied. "His work was his salvation."

*

WILBERT BEGAN TO SETTLE DOWN after the fire scare. He was planning on adding a third bedroom in the upstairs of the house so that four-year-old Jessie could have her own room. Then Pete, who was two years old, and five-month-old Daniel would have a boys' bedroom. It would be best to move Daniel's cot from Liza and Wilbert's room and give them some privacy.

Although the years of arduous labour had exhausted Wilbert and Liza both, they now had a half-acre garden space, free of stumps from the many fallen trees. They had worked the rocky soil with picks and shovels, and a plow pulled behind the horse. The vegetables and berry bushes were flourishing. Along with the garden, the barn had been completed, and the healthy milk cows had a comfortable stall.

At night, when the children were sleeping, Wilbert and Liza chatted about how content they were in their home. Liza looked up from her evening knitting and smiled at Wilbert. "I'm so glad to be here. Aren't you? Have you noticed how much food Pete and Jessie eat?"

"Ya, they want to eat all day. Who could resist your cooking?"

"And they sleep well after all the work they help with."

"Good thing we have them to help with the weeding," agreed Wilbert.

Most important in Wilbert's life was his family, and although he didn't often say it, he was proud of his daughter and sons. When he looked at Jessie, he saw Liza's energy and innocent trust in others. Jessie wanted to be like her mom and insisted that Liza braid her hair just the way Liza often did her own hair. Wilbert loved her eagerness to be helpful. She was a strong girl for her age.

Wilbert liked to see Pete following him around the yard. A quiet boy, Pete was able to help with milking the cow, much to his pleasure. He thought Liza was a fine mother, so efficient and caring, as well as being vigorous and positive about facing challenges. Wilbert wasn't sure how to be a father except to copy his own father: not much talking, strict about manners and getting the work done, and being loyal to his family.

Daniel, a thriving five-month-old, was now olicky, and not a good night sleeper. His eyes were striking, having rapidly changed from the typical blue of a newborn to a deep, dark brown. Even the other children remarked on the darkness of his eyes.

While relaxing over afternoon tea after a busy morning with the children, Millie turned to Gertrude and said softly, "Did you notice Daniel's eyes? Not like Wilbert's or Liza's. I always thought babies were supposed to look like the dad."

Whispering in response, Gertrude commented, "When I got the mail, I heard the neighbour, Mrs. Filipek, say she wondered who the father of that baby really was." The two looked up as Liza came into the room and smiled to greet her, both fidgeting and looking guilty, and then quickly made an excuse that it was time to go back to Thomas and Rose's house to make dinner.

August 30, 1922

~

The next day in his kitchen, Thomas was preparing to go to work with Wilbert and muttered under his breath, "That lazy weakling had better be ready when I get there. I don't want to waste my time waiting for him to eat breakfast again. Too fond of his cozy bed with his wife."

Gertrude, eyes blazing, whirled around from the stove and confronted him angrily. "What do you mean lazy? My brother never stops working. The reason he can keep working long days is the good breakfast he eats. You should take a lesson!"

Millie overheard the comments and stood in front of Thomas, glowering at him. "And I've noticed how you put your hands on Liza when Wilbert can't see, and how you pull her shoulders so she looks at you."

He stomped to the door with a furious scowl, put on his boots, and then retorted, "You two busybodies don't know what you're talking about. It's about time you went away."

After the loud argument, the sisters, insulted by Thomas's comments, packed their cases and moved to Wilbert and Liza's that afternoon. They charged up the hill, breathing heavily from the hike. Liza, sewing in the parlour, was surprised to see them with their cases and said curiously, "What are you doing? Do you think you'll stay here now?"

The words came spurting out of Gertrude, "Thomas is impossible!"

Then Millie said, "He says you and Wilbert are lazy and don't get enough work done! We can't stay there anymore."

Wilbert had quietly entered the kitchen carrying a milk bucket. He listened from behind the door, a wave of alarm building inside him.

"And we told him to keep his hands off you. He thinks he owns you!" screeched Millie.

Memories invaded Wilbert's mind of seeing Thomas standing in the kitchen with his large hands holding Liza's shoulders; of noticing Thomas sneaking glances at Liza during dinners at the flats; of Thomas whispering in Liza's ear when Rose wasn't looking . . .

Liza, speechless, rushed into the bedroom and slammed the door. Wilbert began to smoulder with images of the creeping fury that had haunted his life. He remembered a time when he entered the kitchen at Thomas's house. Thomas had his hands on Liza's waist, and she pushed him back before she rushed out of the room, ignoring Wilbert. Thomas pretended Wilbert wasn't there. Wilbert was left in confusion, not wanting to believe what he'd seen. The returning memory spread eerily in his mind. The many insinuations of Wilbert's weaknesses compared to Thomas's strengths broiled. Over and over, Wilbert heard the screaming words of his sister: "He thinks he owns you!"

Wilbert dropped the bucket and stumbled outside. He marched to the barn, panting and not sure where he was going. His adrenalin pushed him to clamber up the hill behind the house and into the forest, where he continued until he collapsed with angry exhaustion. Consumed with heat and jealous rage, he tried to think. *Thomas is always a bully. I do most of the work, and he bosses people around.* Lying back on the debris-cluttered forest floor, he closed his eyes and willed himself to close his mind to Thomas.

118

THE DISTANCE

Around him were sounds of busy robins and squirrels. When he opened his eyes, he saw the broad wings and white head of an eagle as it circled over the treetops. Almost hidden on a towering larch was a strong-looking osprey nest, and inside was a small bird calling for its parent. The eagle had spied an opportunity for a meal and dived for the nest just as the female osprey appeared, streaming upward behind the eagle and shrieking as it burst down upon the larger bird. The attack by the osprey from straight above knocked the eagle into a branch. Stunned, the eagle collected itself and flew away without the usual strong control characteristic of the majestic bird. As Wilbert watched, he was enthralled to see the osprey get the advantage over the eagle and began to think about how he might gain an advantage over Thomas. He began to feel more confidence in himself and returned to the house.

Liza, Millie, and Gertrude were in the kitchen trying to keep busy by preparing food. Wilbert spat out vehemently, "I have to defend myself against Thomas. He has robbed me of my honour. I'll show him that I'm stronger than him!"

"But Wilbert, what do you mean?" stammered Liza.

Gertrude questioned timidly, "What are you going to do? You can't be thinking of confronting him! You'll never get away with it."

The women were terrified with his insistence that he had to take control but didn't know what to say or do. Liza tried to follow him and calm him down. "We need to ignore Thomas. I'm afraid of him. And I'm afraid you'll get hurt. He's so strong!" Wilbert shrugged her hand off his shoulder and walked outside again.

Wilbert paced, circling the house all night long, his heart a thumping drum in his chest, the backs of his eyes pressured and aching. There was no possibility of even thinking about sleep. He knew the dream would return and Thomas's taunts would beat at him. In the dim early morning

119

light, he pulled his polished Winchester .33 rifle from its shelf in the barn and strode resolutely down the wagon road to Thomas's house.

As he walked, he repeated over and over, through gritted teeth, "He stole my honour. I must defend myself." The rage inside his head obliterated the sounds of his boots crashing through the debris on the trail. Bloodless fingers clenched the rifle barrel. A white-tailed deer bolted in front of him and raced away. His eyes, narrowed with intention, barely noticed. A murder of black crows circled over his head, cawing loudly to each other.

"He stole my honour. He stole my honour." The words being forced from his mouth began to slow his breathing. He stopped and listened. No sounds were coming from Thomas's house.

He muttered to himself, "I know he'll come out at first light to milk the cow. If I hide in the shed, he won't see me." He sat against the wall and waited and waited, feeling the heat in his brain, while he tried to push his heart down in his throat. Finally, in the full daylight, he heard the door of the house open, and he stood up, watching Thomas's unknowing approach. *Stole my honour . . . defend myself.* The drum beat relentlessly. He thought it so loud it would surely warn Thomas.

Thomas leisurely strode toward the cow shed, coming close to the door where Wilbert hid. With careful precision, Wilbert aimed the rifle just as he'd been taught by Thomas years ago. With a galloping heart, Wilbert struggled to keep the rifle level. As he pulled the trigger, fiery words shot from Wilbert's lips, "You stole my honour!" The force of the rifle shot jolted his shoulder. Acrid smoke filled his nostrils and seared his tongue.

The crack of the rifle shot split the air and Thomas' body was ripped open. The bullet shattered his heart in two. Red rivers burst from his chest. Wilbert's eyes bugged out of his face as he watched the scene.

THE DISTANCE

Thomas looked at Wilbert and felt the hate in Wilbert's eyes as he heard the crack of the shot. He caught his breath as if holding it could stop the impact. He felt his body rip open as the bullet shattered his heart in two. Trickles of red quickened into streams of blood flowing down his chest. He wanted to cry out, but his voice was strangled. His body reacted to the force of the rifle shot, and he spun around, his panicked mind screaming No! He stumbled, shaking, his will lifting one foot after the other to run. Spinning, he hurtled thirty yards in the opposite direction. He pushed his feet into the bushes, hearing the snap of the dry branches and thinking desperately, *Faster . . . he can't stop me . . . been through this before . . . not the end.* But the blood had become a river, and his strength was seeping out onto the ground. His body, in slow motion, collapsed into the pool of red. The sticky, slimy feel covered his arms and neck. He struggled to keep his face high; everywhere he looked, he saw red bushes and grass. Thomas faintly heard Wilbert's footsteps as he followed through the leaves and brush, deliberately pushing aside anything in his way, his boots pounding—thump, thump, thump on the ground. *Maybe this really is the end . . . don't feel much pain . . . hard to breathe . . . he'll never kill, me he's too gutless . . .* Thomas sensed Wilbert aiming the rifle at him.

With careful aim, Wilbert shot him once, twice, then three times in the back. Thomas's body jerked violently and convulsed with spasms. When the quivering ended, Wilbert knew the task was finished. Slowly backing away to the wagon road, Wilbert put the rifle over his shoulder and began the hike up the mountain to his home. He looked over his shoulder to see Rose, wakened by the sounds of shooting, racing from the house, calling for Thomas. She screamed at the sight of the lifeless body. He kept climbing up the watchful mountain to his house.

JUDY POLLARD

Wilbert's mission was complete. His nemesis would never steal his honour again. He had defended himself and his family. And he would face the consequences.

September 1922

~

*L*iza jolted awake when she heard Daniel's early morning grunts and squeals. They'd both had a restless night, with her imagining what Wilbert might do about Thomas, and the five-month-old baby fussing, complaining, and not comfortable. He always seemed to sense his mother's distress and responded with uneasy sleep.

She quickly checked the bed beside her for any signs of Wilbert. She jumped up and peered in every room. No signs of Wilbert. Barely breathing, she raced outside to check the outhouse and barn. The realization that he hadn't been home all night churned her stomach.

Returning to the house, she banged the kitchen door and called out, "Gertrude, Millie, wake up! Wilbert is gone. He must be at Thomas's. And the rifle is gone. I have to find him."

The two sisters stumbled into the kitchen, eyes wide. "No, you must stay here. It's not safe," said Gertrude.

Millie nodded in agreement. Both women were aware of how furious their brother had been the day before. "We have to keep the children safe. I hear Jessie talking to Pete. Pete is calling for you."

Liza, grabbing her jacket, pleaded with the women, tears escaping from bloodshot eyes, "Please just tell them I'm looking for the cow. Daniel is still in his cot. I nursed him in the night. Maybe you could try giving him some cow's milk with the new baby bottle you brought from Switzerland."

They hesitated but nodded agreement. Gertrude went upstairs and Millie to the bedroom to care for Daniel. Liza, barely dressed, ran down the path. Just then she saw Wilbert, trudging toward her, rifle over his shoulder. His blood-splattered face was a hard mask, his teeth set in determination. His eyes stared at the ground ahead. Streaks of red were splashed across his shirt and the broad suspenders. The realization that something very bad had happened hit Liza with the force of a whip.

"Wilbert, where have you been? You don't look like yourself!" Liza said loudly as she stood blocking his way.

"I had to defend my honour," Wilbert muttered and tried to move past her.

She put her hands firmly on his arms. "Wilbert, what did you do?"

"I had to stop him. He will never steal from me again!"

Liza, totally aghast, pushed Wilbert to make him sit down on a stump. Her body was shaking. A vise tightened around her chest; she struggled to talk. "Tell me Wilbert. Tell me!"

Wilbert sat, head hanging. He finally answered, "I shot him. Thomas won't bother us again."

Liza shrieked, "No, no, no!" Crushing waves of terror squeezed inside her. "You shot him? You're a gentle man. You couldn't kill someone!"

The two sat—Liza sobbed and Wilbert slumped—staring at the ground. They barely noticed the sound of somebody coming up the wagon road. Hanna, breathing heavily, suddenly stood in front of them, staring at Wilbert. "What the heck is going on? Rose says you shot Thomas! You better give me that rifle," he commanded.

Wilbert got to his feet. With shoulders slumped, he offered the rifle to Hanna. "He stole my honour," he mumbled.

THE DISTANCE

Hanna took the rifle from Wilbert and led the heavy-hearted pair to their now empty house. The house was quiet because Gertrude and Millie had left with the children and some food and gone to the beach. Wilbert didn't have much more to say except that he would wait to talk to the police. Liza caught glimpses of his blood-spattered face out of the corner of her eye but couldn't bring herself to actually look at him. She could tell that he was totally unaware of his appearance and exhausted as he sat in his corner chair.

Liza had no words. Inside her head was a storm of colliding thoughts. *My husband shot him? He could not kill a person. It's wrong. Did Thomas attack him?* She silently crept into her bedroom and buried herself under the bedcovers.

Finally, in the evening the police officer arrived. He looked official in his dark blue uniform with the single row of shiny buttons up the front and the high collar at his neck. He tried to persuade Wilbert to explain the details of what happened, but Wilbert was taciturn, simply repeating his confession, saying he had waited in the shed for Thomas to come out to milk the cow, and then shot him. Because of the lateness in the day, the police officer stayed at the house with Wilbert overnight, deciding to wait for the arrival of the coroner on the boat from Kaslo the next day.

Gertrude, Millie, and the children quietly returned and stayed away from the scene in the sitting room. Gertrude suspected that Liza must be in her room and left her alone for the night, not sure if she knew that Wilbert and the officer were still there. They took the children upstairs to read stories and settle them for the night, and then squeezed into bed with Jessie and Pete.

The next morning, Liza went out the back door and wandered into the garden, too frightened to find out what was happening with Wilbert.

125

She was sure they were still in the house somewhere. High above her, the early sun was brilliant. The garden and tidy house were illuminated with warmth. It seemed as perfect as she wanted it to be. But her mind was haunted with the anguish of knowing perfection was lost. The morning breeze down the mountainside brushed her tears, and she breathed its rich fragrance, attempting to relieve the darkness inside her soul. She straightened her dress and pulled her hair back into the bun on her neck.

The kitchen door opened, and she saw Wilbert still wearing the same shirt. He looked no different than he had the day before when he trudged up the path. Sprayed blood, now blackened, still covered his chest and his thick suspenders. Wilbert insisted on shaving every morning, even if he only went outside to work, but now his face was covered in stubble, sweat, and dried blood.

Compared to Wilbert, the police officer looked composed and clean, although unshaven. He put on his peaked cap and came out, getting ahead of Wilbert and tugging on the handcuffs that joined them. They both stumbled as Wilbert tried to get down the steps in leg chains. The short chain between metal ankle cuffs made it hazardous to move his feet.

Liza called out, "How can he walk like that? He'll get hurt!"

"Well, okay," said the officer. "I'll take the chains off for now. Guess he won't run far. And here comes Hanna in the wagon. He's got the coroner with him. He'll help me keep Wilbert in line. When we get him in the wagon, I'll put the leg chains back on."

Liza ran to Wilbert and tried to grab his arm while the officer was taking off the chains. "Wilbert, you have to talk to me. What did you say? What's happening? When will you talk to me?" she shouted in his face. Wilbert stared with vacant eyes. Darkness in his face showed the lack of rest; he was resigned to being led away. The officer pushed on his elbow as Wilbert clambered into the wagon. Liza stood in front of the officer and demanded, "Where are you taking him?"

"I'm taking Wilbert on the boat to Kaslo. He'll be charged with the murder of Thomas Rochat." He looked her in the eye, and continued, "He'll be in jail in Kaslo until the hearing, and then he'll go to the Nelson jail until the trial."

She couldn't believe her ears, and stammered, "What? How long will it take?"

"Don't know till the court dates get set." He shrugged.

"What am I going to do? We need him here. When can he come back?"

"Don't know Mrs. Jeanneret. Can't say. This is murder," he commented unemotionally. He moved her aside and climbed on the wagon.

"Wilbert, you have to at least say goodbye. When will I see you? What will we do?" she beseeched. Liza collapsed on the grass, banging her fists on the grass. "This can't be real. They can't take him away!"

The wagon disappeared around the corner just as Gertrude, having overheard, bustled over to Liza and threw her arms around her shoulders. They sobbed together.

"Liza, we will find out. There must be a way to see him." Liza, now inconsolable, shook her head.

The sounds of children running from the house made Liza sit up and look around. Gertrude muttered resolutely, "We need to be brave for the children," as she handed Liza a handkerchief.

Liza wiped her eyes and tried to look less teary as she greeted Jessie and Pete, "Did you have your breakfast? Where is Aunt Millie?" Jessie, looking shocked to see her mother's streaked face and bloodshot eyes, responded, "She's feeding Daniel. He's very cranky today."

Pete tried to push his way onto Liza's lap, but Gertrude pulled him over to sit with her. She explained to the children, "Papa has gone away for a while. Mama is very sad. We must all help with the chores. You know Papa will be happy if you do."

Jessie and Pete gazed at Liza, knowing something was very wrong. They nodded in agreement. Jessie said, "Pete, let's go take the cow to the pasture." The two children slowly left, each taking a look back at their mother with confused faces and wrinkled brows. Liza felt relieved that she didn't need to try to explain more to them.

Liza moaned, "There is so much work. How can we do it without him?"

"The best way is to get started," said Gertrude as she stood up and pulled Liza to her feet. They dragged themselves up the steps to kitchen to find Millie and Daniel. It was impossible for Liza to push the thoughts from her mind. *We can't survive without him, even if he is guilty. My children's lives are ruined. They will have no father.*

*

I WATCHED HANS'S FACE AS he began to comprehend the impacts on the Jeanneret family of what had happened. Finally, he couldn't restrain himself any longer and burst out, "This story is so tragic!"

I explained, "When I first heard about the murder I read several newspaper reports describing the people involved and their backgrounds. I also overheard many rumours about what must have happened. I'm so fascinated with the story that I can't get it out of my mind. The details as I recount them to you are my interpretations. However, this was undoubtedly an extremely serious situation for the Jeanerets. And there's more to the story yet. The trial was epic and precedent setting. Shall I go on?"

"Oh, please continue," urged Hans.

"The trial took place in the Nelson Courthouse in October 1922."

October 1922, Nelson Courthouse
~

"*I* rushed through the dark, heavily panelled doors of the courthouse, managing to squeeze between others crowding in and quietly moving forward until I was in the courtroom. There was a space in the front row of the gallery—the best view. That was a relief because even with steel-rimmed glasses, my vision wasn't good when it came to making out facial expressions from a distance. I was not going to take a chance on missing any details of the trial, especially after I had completed the arduous row all the way to Argenta and back. When I was there, I had been able to walk around the area of the murder and the hamlet, thus developing a theory of what happened. There had been many newspaper articles with descriptions of the site; however, experiencing it for myself was important.

"With people crowded into all the seats, the room was a hum of secretive voices. I kept quiet, watching, listening, and thinking. The consequences of Jeannert being found guilty were horrendous. He would undoubtedly be sentenced to death. That would seem to be a great shame. From what I had found out from newspaper reports, Jeanneret was an educated and thoughtful businessman who had personally contributed money to start a small community school in Argenta—not the reputation one would expect of a person accused of murder.

"The situation for Mrs. Jeanneret seemed desperate. If her husband were found guilty, even if by some miracle of mercy he was sentenced to prison for the rest of his life, she would be left with nothing and would not have a way to support her children or herself. The land on which their house and barn were located was legally owned by Wilbert. If he had a will and named her as the benefactor of the property, she would then have legal ownership. As a widow, she had few legal rights, and right of ownership was questionable. A law regarding the right of a woman to enter into legal agreements and own property has only recently been established in British Columbia. I was eager for proceedings to start."

Nelson Courthouse

THE TRIAL

~

Proceedings Begin

Wilbert squinted against the sharp sunlight pouring through the high windows of the Supreme Court. For six weeks he had lived in the dim light of a basement jail cell. His body had become stiffened by the severe cold walls of the cell and the rock-hard bed. Despite his attempts to stop the contortions of dread in his mind, he felt emptied of any ability to find lightness. Now he wanted to look outside to see trees and bushes, but the windows were below the eaves of the tall building and revealed only sky and light. Firm hands of the jail guards led him to the prisoner box where he would sit with his back to the restless crowd in the viewing galleries. He hobbled slowly with the leg chains on his ankles, and his hands, cuffed in front, were forced into an awkward prayer pose. He shuffled to the box, eyes fixed on the floorboards.

Both guards were imposing figures, close to six feet tall and dressed in dark uniforms, with an official crest on the shoulder and a firearm in their belts. Their faces were serious and their eyes expressionless, yet they gave the impression of sharp alertness to everything around them, most especially Wilbert's behaviour.

JUDY POLLARD

Wilbert's box faced the raised judge's bench, which dominated the room and stretched almost all the way across the imposing dark panelled wall. Even the judge's chair seemed abnormally tall, and above it, the brightly coloured crest of the Province of British Columbia decorated the wall. Above his head, Wilbert saw strong wooden beams stretching across the high ceiling and felt the air movement caused by the large fans.

Wilbert was dressed in the best clothes he had brought from Switzerland, wool slacks and his expensive Harris Tweed jacket, which discreetly concealed the curved spine between his shoulders. He hadn't worn this clothing since his wedding in 1914, and he felt his biceps squeezed into the jacket, especially with his hands cuffed forward. Immediately in front of his box, Wilbert saw two large oak tables—one for the Crown counsel and one for the defence lawyer. The jury box, with the twelve jury members seated in two rows, was situated along the right wall of the room. Just beneath the judge's bench and in front of the defence counsel was the witness stand.

Even with his back to the room, Wilbert could feel the heat and rustle of people pressed into the Supreme Court for his murder trial. They wanted to see the villain in handcuffs and leg chains. The pounding in his chest drowned out the hubbub. Finally, when he was seated, the handcuffs were removed, releasing his stiffened fingers and wrists. A guard stood at the entrance to the box, while the other sat against the wall in order to survey the room. No matter where the guards stood, Wilbert continued to feel the sharp eyes riveting him to his chair.

It was 9:00 a.m. on Monday, October 12, 1922. By 9:15, the gallery overflowed with people from all around Kootenay Lake filling every pew. There was a buzz of high-pitched comments about the story and about the possible penalties. Some in the crowd had even witnessed a hanging in Nelson about twenty years earlier, and one person said with

134

a self-important tone, "There could be another hanging in the courtyard. I helped build the scaffolding, and I saw the whole thing. I watched the guy lurch around at the end of the rope." The gasps of horror from those around him were easily overheard in the room.

A balcony above seated another thirty people. The journalists sat in a sectioned off area near the front of the other floor seating. People who couldn't find seats leaned against the wall. All were fidgeting and gossiping. They had heard rumours. "Did you know that he came from Switzerland and speaks French?" "I heard he lives at the north end of Kootenay Lake, past Kaslo, and has never been seen in Nelson before." "He killed his work partner. They came from Europe together."

Afraid to look behind him, Wilbert yearned to know if Liza and his sister Gertrude had found a seat before the crowd pushed in. Gertrude had visited him in jail, brought him clean clothes, and reassured him that Millie was staying in Argenta to care for the children. The three women had agreed that Gertrude would accompany Liza through the trial. He wondered if Liza would really come, knowing that she was worried about people pointing and staring at her.

*

I COMMENTED TO HANS, "I wondered about Liza's reflections on the events, her emotional losses, and her choices about securing the future for herself and her children. As a woman, she had little power and financial stability without a husband, so might she have felt trapped and unable to do anything other than be the obedient hard-working wife. What was her opinion of Wilbert when he became a murderer? Could she have found him threatening?"

*

JUDY POLLARD

GERTRUDE AND LIZA GENTLY PUSHED forward in the crowd and sat behind the journalists. Gertrude whispered, "Just looking at the judge's bench makes me nervous."

Liza replied, "Me too. Wilbert looks shrunken beside those tall police. He seems helpless. Did you hear what people are saying about him? I thought I heard somebody talk about a hanging in the courtyard. I'm so scared! My mind is going crazy!"

Gertrude put her hand on Liza's arm and said in a calming whisper, "We are here together. We must keep faith that we will all get through this."

Liza glanced at Gertrude's gentle face and saw the determination in her eyes. She said softly, "I know. I'm so grateful you are here. And I know Wilbert is also thankful."

As Wilbert waited with trepidation in the prisoner box, it gave him a small amount of comfort to know that the building was constructed with select marble from the Marblehead Quarry, only a few miles from his home. The emotion-laden room was beginning to close in around him. Odours of stale cigar smoke, combined with already sweating bodies, seemed to soak up the oxygen. He craned his neck and peered over his shoulder, searching for Liza and Gertrude. *Oh, I see them near the front row. Gertrude is whispering in Liza's ear and patting her arm. Liza's been crying. Gertrude will look after her even when I can't. At least Rose has gone to the cousins in Trail.*

The court bailiff entered and stood looking at the crowd. "Sorry folks. If you don't have a seat, you'll have to leave," he announced. This was met by grumbles, but those standing filed out the door.

Bailiff Armstrong called, "All rise. This court is in session." Judge Stanley swept through the side door, his imposing black robe parading behind him and showing off the apple-red rectangular collar decorating

136

his back. At his throat, the pointed white shirt collar held in place the inverted V-shaped white tabs which hung down his chest almost to his waist. Judge Stanley's face was narrow, with a long, hooked nose and penetrating dark eyes that often communicated his expectations and displeasure. The top of his head had a billiard ball-like sheen, making him even more austere in appearance.

Everybody stood and acknowledged the judge as he entered and then silently sat down after he took his place at the bench. The court clerk announced, "Chief Justice Douglas Stanley is presiding in the case of *Regina vs. Jeanneret*, file number 1922, BCJ. No. 87."

A loud whisper could be heard in the crowd, "Who's Regina?"

The hushed reply carried through the silence, "The Monarchy."

The Crown and defence attorneys were asked to approach the bench. Mr. Angus, the defence attorney, was short like Wilbert. With his floor-length black robe and flowing scalloped edged sleeves, he had the appearance of a charging bull. Thick, dark, oiled hair was plastered back on his head, framing his round face and set jaw. The Crown attorney, Mr. Renard, was the opposite, with a narrow face and pointed chin. He was tall and stiff, with bony arms protruding from the sleeves of his robe. There was a sharpness about his look that Wilbert felt viscerally. Both attorneys conferred briefly with the judge before taking seats at their respective tables.

Judge Douglas Stanley recounted that the jury members had been selected earlier. The twelve members were from a group of local property owners, all married family men from various professional and business backgrounds. None of them had any knowledge of Wilbert previously. It was apparent that observers in the galleries recognized many of them as they murmured approval when each one was confirmed by the Crown prosecutor and the lawyer for the defence.

JUDY POLLARD

Judge Stanley addressed the accused in a loud voice, "Wilbert Jeanneret of Argenta, BC, you are charged with the murder of Thomas Rochat, also of Argenta, BC. The charge of murder is defined as a premeditated act and, in such cases, the province is allowed to seek the death penalty. How do you plead: guilty or not guilty?"

Wilbert stood and looked directly at the judge. "I plead self-defence, Your Honour." He spoke in English. Whispers could be heard amongst the crowd.

Judge Stanley said, "You have chosen to remain mute on the question of guilty or not guilty. I must inform you that remaining mute is interpreted by the court as a plea of not guilty and is recorded as such. A jury of your peers has been selected. The case for the Crown will be presented first by the Crown attorney. When that presentation is completed, you may present your defence."

Wilbert nodded in understanding and sat down.

138

The Case for the Prosecution

~

"Mr. Renard, please proceed with your case," said Judge Stanley.

Mr. Renard rose at his table and addressed the Judge. "Your Honour, I will be presenting indisputable evidence that Mr. Jeanneret did indeed murder Mr. Rochat on August 31, as charged. I will bring forward several witnesses to testify, including the arresting police officer, the coroner, and residents of Argenta. The witnesses will testify that Mr. Jeanneret, becoming infuriated that Mr. Rochat had criminal association with Mrs. Jeanneret, first threatened Mr. Rochat with his shotgun and told him to leave the country. Then the next day, he returned early in the morning with his rifle and shot and killed Mr. Rochat. The first witness to be called is the BC Provincial Police Officer who attended the scene, Constable Oland."

The bailiff, waiting in the hall with the witness, led him to the witness stand. The court clerk held out the Bible and said, "Constable Oland please place your hand on the Bible. Do you swear to tell the truth and nothing but the truth, so help you God?"

"I do," the constable said, sounding nervous in contrast to the appearance of calm authority provided by his dark police uniform. He had never testified in a trial before.

139

"Please say and spell your first and last name for the record," said the court clerk. The constable did so. Mr. Renard stood before the witness box and asked the Constable to tell the court what happened on September 1, 1922.

Constable Oland explained, "I was in Kaslo the afternoon of September 1 and received a telegram from Howser to go immediately to Argenta as there had been a murder. The victim was identified as Mr. Rochat and the murderer as Mr. Jeanneret. I arrived by boat in the evening and went directly to the home of Mr. Jeanneret. He was waiting for me. I cautioned and arrested him, saying he would be charged with murder. He offered his shotgun and rifle to me of his own volition, and I placed them in a location where I could ensure they were secure. I also attached leg chains to his ankles to prevent him from trying to escape."

Mr. Renard, with a sharp tone, questioned, "Was there anything unusual about the conversation you had at the time with Mr. Jeanneret?"

"Yes, there was. He handed me a written statement that he had prepared while he was waiting for me to arrive."

"Do you have that statement with you?"

"Yes."

"Please read it now."

"Yes, I will read it. 'I heard him coming out of his house at about seven o'clock, and as I was stepping out of the shop, he was ten feet away from me. I shot him, he started to run, and I shot again. I regret deeply having rendered my sister a widow, but then she had only one child to my wife's three babies, and it was one of us that had to go.'" Constable Oland looked up and added, "I was surprised at his honesty and sincerity." The attorney accepted the note and with a brief nod, offered it to the court clerk.

THE DISTANCE

Mr. Renard said, "Your Honour, I would like this note, signed by Mr. Jeanneret, to be admitted as evidence and numbered as exhibit one for the record."

Judge Stanley directed the court clerk to hand him the note, initialled it, and returned it to the clerk to be entered as an exhibit. Wilbert sat patiently waiting for the judge to finish. He caught the eye of Mr. Angus, and the two exchanged resigned looks.

Mr. Renard asked, "What happened next, Constable Oland?"

Speaking in a flat tone, the Constable gave his explanation. "Because of the lateness in the evening, I stayed in the parlour of the Jeanneret home with him, waiting for the arrival of the coroner in the morning. Mr. Jeanneret was quiet and compliant. We spent the night in chairs on opposite sides of the room. In the morning, at my request, a neighbour, Mr. Hanna, brought his horse-drawn wagon to the house to transport Mr. Jeanneret to the wharf. The coroner arrived and, after examining the body, joined us in the boat to take Mr. Jeanneret to the jail in Kaslo to await a preliminary hearing. The body of Mr. Rochat was taken to the morgue in Kaslo in a different boat."

Mr. Renard said, "I have here a box containing a shotgun and a second box containing a rifle. I will ask you to identify these items separately." He handed the shotgun to the constable and asked if that was the same gun given to him by Mr. Jeanneret. The constable affirmed that to be true.

"Your Honour, I request that this shotgun be labelled as evidence and admitted as an exhibit for the record." The gun was taken by the clerk and handed to the judge to examine.

"Clerk, please label and mark this shotgun as exhibit two and enter it into the court record," said the judge.

JUDY POLLARD

"Thank you, Your Honour." Mr. Renard lifted the rifle from its box. "Constable Oland, is this the rifle you were given by Mr. Jeanneret?"

The constable examined it and nodded. "Yes, this is the Winchester .33 that was given to me and that he said was the gun he used to shoot Mr. Rochat."

Mr. Renard handed the gun to the clerk and said, "Your Honour, I request that this rifle be labelled as evidence and admitted as an exhibit for the record." Again, the clerk gave the weapon to the judge who carefully examined it before he returned it and instructed that it be labelled as exhibit three.

"Thank you, Your Honour," said Mr. Renard, "Constable Oland, do you have anything further to add?"

"No, sir."

Mr. Renard said, "Your Honour, I have completed initial questioning of this witness." As he returned to his table to await the cross-examination, he glanced at Mr. Angus with a smirk on his face. Obviously the Crown attorney thought this was an easy case for him to win. Wilbert noticed the sarcastic look and hunched his shoulders with despair. It had been tempting to block out the words during the constable's testimony, but it didn't work; he was aware that painful as it was to hear the story told, it was important for him to listen and identify any discrepancies to his attorney.

Judge Stanley asked, "Mr. Angus, do you wish to cross-examine this witness?"

Mr. Angus answered, "Yes, Your Honour." He rose and stood in front of the witness box. "Constable Oland, did you at any time think that Mr. Jeanneret was not being truthful?"

"No, sir," said the constable.

142

THE DISTANCE

"Did you at any time believe he was a further threat to you or anybody else?"

"No, sir."

"Thank you. That is all my questions, Your Honour."

"Mr. Renard, is the testimony of Constable Oland complete?" asked the judge.

"Yes, Your Honour, although I may want to have him return to the witness stand later in the trial."

"Very well." After noting the time, Judge Stanley announced that there would be a lunch break and stood to leave the bench.

"All rise," said the court clerk. Everybody rose while the judge departed the court. The room emptied with a buzz of conversation. The guards steered Wilbert back to the chilly cell for his meagre lunch; another meal he wouldn't eat.

Gertrude and Liza slipped out of the room and sat on the grass in the sunshine at the back of the courthouse. As usual, Gertrude was prepared and offered Liza a sandwich. Liza, her face twisted with worry, shook her head. "No, thank you. My stomach won't let me eat. I wish I could run away. I don't want to listen anymore."

Gertrude nodded. "I feel the same way. This must be so hard for Wilbert, and he has to just sit and listen, just like us. Let's go for a walk and get away from these other people. Nobody seems to know who we are, so that's a relief."

When the court resumed after lunch, everybody took their previous places. The bailiff announced, "All rise. The court is in session," and the judge entered. He bowed and sat down. All the others in the room waited for his signal before sitting. Wilbert returned to the prisoner box and sat with hands calmly on the table, listening attentively.

143

"Mr. Renard, please continue with your submissions," said Judge Stanley.

"Thank you, Your Honour. I wish to submit another document written by Mr. Jeanneret. Five days after the arrest of Mr. Jeanneret, he attended a preliminary hearing in Kaslo. After being duly cautioned about the possibility of incriminating himself, he insisted on presenting a second detailed statement, noting that he presented the statement without his wife's knowledge."

Wilbert's shoulder slumped as he suspected what was coming next. He didn't know if his attorney was aware of the other note he had written. He was sure that Liza knew nothing about it, and icy fingers clenched his heart. *Would this be too hard for her to hear?*

Mr. Renard read the statement as follows:

> I felt that as long as he lived, I could not care for my wife any more, although I never had any doubt she was innocent, so I killed him, and although I have been tormented with remorse ever since on account of his wife and relatives in Trail, I feel the regained love of my wife and three little children is worth anything that I have to pay for it. Rochat told my wife once that he had seen me coming against his house with a gun and was sure it was to kill him. Also, on the night of his death, even after I had given him a week's notice, he said to his wife he felt sure I was going to shoot him in the morning. This shew that he would have done it if he were in my place, and for him, like for me, there was only one possible way to redeem one's woman's honour.

144

THE DISTANCE

Liza and Gertrude sat touching shoulders and listening intently. The two of them carefully avoided doing anything that might draw attention to them. From around them, they could hear whispers wondering if Mrs. Jeanneret was there and what she looked like. Confused embarrassment overwhelmed her. Her body was shaking. *What were people thinking of her?* She felt desperate to get out of the room. Gertrude held her arm and forced her to stay seated, so Liza tried to shrink her body into the bench seat.

The crowd in the galleries burst into whispered comments. Even though they tried to keep voices low, the eruption of surprise overwhelmed the cavernous courtroom. Judge Stanley pounded his gavel and commanded, "Order in court. Be quiet. Mr. Renard please continue."

The Crown attorney waited for quiet before he said in a self-satisfied tone, "Your Honour, I wish to have this document, written and signed by Mr. Jeanneret, labelled as evidence and placed as exhibit four for the court record." The paper was given to the judge. Before initialling it, he read it carefully, seeming to look for any possibility that it might not be genuine. When he was satisfied, he returned it to the clerk and confirmed that it was exhibit four.

"Mr. Renard, do you have anything further to say on this item?"

"No, Your Honour."

"Mr. Angus, you may ask questions of Mr. Renard regarding the note he has read."

"I have no questions at this time, Your Honour," said Mr. Angus, as he stood at his table, his face contorted and frowning as he processed the written evidence that had been presented. "I was not aware of the note, so I will need time to prepare my thoughts."

"Very well. We will break for today and resume the case for the prosecution at 9:30 in the morning."

145

Again the court clerk stood and said, "All rise." The judge left the chamber and everybody in the galleries whispered as they pushed their way out the doors, astonished by what they had heard. It was obvious that Wilbert spoke and wrote in English in spite of the rumours. The day had been tedious because of the careful procedures that were followed. They intended to come again the next day, hoping to hear more unexpected information. Liza and Gertrude stayed in their seats until others left and then quietly exited. Wilbert looked over his shoulder, trying to see Liza's face and catch her eye, but she would not look up. Adding to the intensity of the exhausting day was the pain he felt not knowing what Liza was feeling and thinking.

As the jail guards approached, Wilbert sat slumped in the prisoner box. A turmoil of regret, confusion, and fear tore at his being. He knew he was in trouble after the way his admissions of guilt were read in court. And the next day might be even worse. The piercing ridges of the handcuffs were tightened on his wrists while the guards lifted his elbows to force him to stand. As they walked toward the doorway, Mr. Angus said quietly to Wilbert, "I'll come to see you in the cell. We'll talk about what to do next."

When Mr. Angus arrived in the cell, Wilbert was dejectedly slumped on the edge of the bed. He jumped up when the cell door clanged open and burst out, "I'm sorry. I know I didn't tell you about that note. I didn't think it would be used in court, and I was more worried about what the coroner would say in his testimony."

"I was surprised to learn about the note, but it can't be helped now. As I question witnesses, I plan to bring the focus back to your good reputation and respectable behaviour in the community, and there will be several people who provide that type of evidence. Now try to relax for the night before we go back into the courtroom tomorrow."

The Case for the Prosecution: Day Two

~

Once again, the courtroom was swathed in brilliant sunlight pouring through the high windows. As he was led through the doorway by the jail guards, Wilbert dropped his gaze to the floor. The leg chains made a soft scraping sound on the wood when he hobbled forward into the prisoner box. In the box, he sat with his arms forward on the table while the guard removed the pinching handcuffs.

He had noticed that the galleries were filled with spectators and suspected that some had been there yesterday. Scanning the front rows, he saw Liza and Gertrude and felt a wave of relief. Liza looked up, and for an instant, her deep blue eyes met his. Her look conveyed such a strong sense of caring as well as trepidation that he instinctively pulled his body more erect. He could feel her strength being directed toward him, and he was grateful.

The testimony today was going to be ugly because Mr. Angus told him that the first witness would be the coroner giving testimony regarding the injuries to Thomas's body. He was relieved to remember that Rose had gone to stay with relatives in Trail immediately after the preliminary inquest, so at least she wouldn't be in the gallery listening to the coroner's descriptions. But he dreaded having to listen himself and hoped Liza could avoid breaking down when she heard the details.

Mr. Angus and Mr. Renard were already seated at their tables. Bailiff Armstrong entered the room and said, "All rise. This court is in session." Judge Stanley energetically swept into the courtroom through the side door. After waiting for the judge to be seated, everybody in the room sat down. The excitement and curiosity of the crowd were tangible after the explosive testimony of the day before.

The court clerk announced the continuation of the case of *Regina vs. Jeanneret*. Judge Stanley nodded to Mr. Renard and said, "You may continue with the case of the prosecution."

Mr. Renard stood and addressed the judge. "Thank you, Your Honour. As my first witness, I will call Dr. Douglas Berclay, who performed the autopsy on Mr. Rochat."

The bailiff accompanied Dr. Berclay to the witness stand. The court clerk held out the Bible and said, "Dr. Berclay, please place your hand on the Bible. Do you swear to tell the truth, so help you God?"

"I do," said Dr. Berclay.

"Please say and spell your first and last name for the record," said the clerk. After Dr. Berclay had done so, Mr. Renard stood and addressed the witness box.

"Dr. Berclay, I understand that you conducted an autopsy on the body of Thomas Rochat of Argenta, is that so?"

"Yes, sir that is true," said Dr. Berclay.

"Please present your report to the court."

"Your Honour, I examined the body of Mr. Rochat in Kaslo on September second, the day after the murder. Mr. Rochat was thirty-nine years of age and in excellent physical condition. He had been shot with a rifle at close range. The first bullet fired from directly in front of him entered the breast, striking the fifth rib, tore through the heart, splitting it in two before it emerged from the right side of the back under the ninth rib. The soft-nosed bullet had spread in a customary fashion and caused a wound that would be fatal. After the initial shot, Mr. Rochat turned and ran approximately thirty yards before collapsing on the ground. His assailant then walked to him and shot him three times in the back, smashing three ribs with the bullet exiting from the left side, cutting the muscle of his left arm. The fact that Mr. Rochat was able to run that distance after the first shot is evidence of his marvellous physique. The bleeding from both wounds would have been profuse. Large pools of blood at the site were reported to me by Constable Oland. Both shots were of a fatal nature."

Mr. Renard thanked Dr. Berclay, and then addressed the judge and said that he was finished with the testimony of this witness. As he sat down at the table, he caught the eye of Mr. Angus and gave him a slightly smug smile as if he considered the testimony to be totally incriminating.

Liza sat like an alabaster statue, with no room in her lungs for breath; her mind flooded with a vision of Thomas's muscular chest and the feeling of his powerful heart throbbing under her tentative fingers. That day years ago, when she had felt herself surrender to his insistence, she was overtaken by the flattery of his desire, even though a murky battle of guilt and fear pushed and pulled inside her. It wasn't possible that his perfect chest could have been torn open and his heart pumped jets of blood! She felt faint and leaned against Gertrude. She knew there would never be a moment in her life when she could release her anguish and acknowledge her feelings for Thomas. If he hadn't saved her from that monster MacLeod, what would have happened to her? And after he saved her, there had been so many changes in both their lives, some happy ones and some webs of complications. She wondered whether she could go on listening to the trial, and yet she knew she had to keep listening.

Judge Stanley looked at the defence lawyer. "Mr. Angus, do you wish to cross-examine this witness?"

Mr. Angus stood and replied that he did. The judge told him to proceed. "Dr. Berclay, you noted that it was remarkable that Mr. Rochat ran a distance of thirty yards after being shot at close range in the chest. Have you even been aware of a similar incident in your experience as a coroner?"

"Yes, sir," replied Dr. Berclay. "I completed an autopsy last year on a man of similar age who had been accidentally shot with a shotgun and who also was able to run approximately twenty yards before collapsing. I know that hunters who shoot wildlife such as deer or bear also report that an animal is able to run a similar distance after being struck by the first bullet. In the case of Mr. Rochat, I am sure he would have died from the initial injury after he fell to the ground, even if the assailant had not followed him and shot him in the back."

"Do you believe it was the same shooter in both instances? Could the shots in the back have been made by a different person?"

"Yes, sir, I believe it was the same shooter. The bullets retrieved from the chest area and the back and arm were all from the same rifle. As well, when Mr. Rochat's wife ran from the house after hearing gunshots, she saw Mr. Jeanneret as he left the property with his rifle and hiked up the path. She testified at the preliminary inquest that she did not see any other people present at the time."

"Thank you, Dr. Berclay." Mr. Angus turned to the judge "Your Honour, that completes my cross-examination of this witness at this time. However, I may wish to recall Dr. Berclay to the stand at a later point."

Throughout the report of the shooting, Wilbert sat head down on the table, replaying the vision of Thomas's chest bursting with blood,

THE DISTANCE

the shriek of shock, the sight of Thomas forcing his body to twist away and his legs pumping forward, red rivers still streaming from his chest. The metallic scent of blood pushed into Wilbert's memory of leaning over the body to deliver the final shots. He was barely aware of the judge speaking.

The judge thanked the witness and told him that he would be taken out of the courtroom in case he might be recalled later in the trial, in order to avoid the possibility that he would be influenced by other witnesses.

Judge Stanley asked the prosecuting attorney, Mr. Renard, to call his next witness, who requested the bailiff to bring Mr. Jones, the Argenta schoolteacher, to the witness stand. Wilbert was surprised to see Mr. Jones as a witness because he thought of him as a friend. Wilbert was part of the hiring committee when the school was started two years ago and had contributed money. Mr. Jones was dressed in a dark charcoal suit, white shirt, and brown tie. His face was tanned from the summer sun, and his grey eyes glanced around the room. Slight worry wrinkles were visible on his forehead. He looked straight into Wilbert's eyes with an apologetic stare. Wilbert returned the look with a resigned sigh.

After he had been sworn in by the court clerk and spelled his name for the court record, Mr. Renard began questioning him. "Mr. Jones, I understand that you have been a resident of Argenta for three years. Please describe your occupation and where you live in relation to the home of Mr. Rochat."

Mr. Jones explained that he had been hired three years previously to develop a small school for the community, and he was the only teacher. The school building and small home were directly across the road and were within sight of the yard surrounding the house of Mr. Rochat.

"Mr. Jones, on the morning of August 31, did you hear any unusual noises?"

"Yes, sir. I heard the shot of a rifle coming from the direction of the Rochat property. As I went outside, I heard Mrs. Rochat screaming and calling her husband's name."

Mr. Renard asked, "What did you do?"

"I ran across the road and found her lying over the body of Mr. Rochat, sobbing uncontrollably. There was a large pool of blood all around the body, and he appeared to be dead. She said that her brother had shot her husband, and she saw him going back up the mountain with his rifle."

Wilbert, listening with an inner groan, was surprised that Mr. Jones had arrived at the yard so soon after he left. *I wish that hadn't happened . . . no wonder he's testifying against me.*

"Please tell the court what happened next," said Mr. Renard.

"I ran to the home of Mr. Filipek and told him that Mr. Rochat was shot. He volunteered to ride the two-hour journey to Howser and send a telegram to the BC Provincial Police in Kaslo asking them to come immediately."

Mr. Renard asked, "What did you do after that?"

"I ran back to try to help Mrs. Rochat and stay with her until other help came. Soon Mr. Hanna came, and we helped her cover the body and stayed with her for most of the day until the police officer was able to come by boat."

Mr. Renard addressed the judge and said that he was finished with the testimony of this witness. Judge Stanley asked Mr. Angus if he wished to cross-examine the witness.

Mr. Angus said, "Yes, thank you, Your Honour." Turning his attention to the witness, he asked, "Mr. Jones how well did you know Mr. Rochat and his wife?"

THE DISTANCE

"I knew them as neighbours and parents of a child in the school. We did not have a particular friendship."

"How well did you know Mr. Jeanneret?"

"Mr. Jeanneret was very involved in the group that created the funds for the school and hired me as the teacher. I had many conversations with him. His oldest child attended some of the school events."

"Did you have reason to believe that Mr. Jeanneret was a violent person?"

"No sir. However, several days before the shooting, I noticed Mr. Jeanneret at the home of Mr. Rochat, and I heard a loud argument. I couldn't understand what was said."

"Did Mr. Jeanneret have his rifle at that time?"

"Not that I could see."

"From your experience, how would you describe Mr. Jeanneret?"

"I found him to be very polite, well-mannered, and calm. He listened carefully when we were planning the schoolroom and although he might be described as taciturn, he added helpful suggestions to the discussion. He was the main financial contributor to the school fund. I understand that he had a reputation as a good businessman."

"What was your thought when Mrs. Rochat called to you that Mr. Rochat was dead at the hand of Mr. Jeanneret and asked for help?"

"I was astonished. I could not imagine Mr. Jeanneret shooting anybody, let alone his business partner. If anything, I think it would be more likely that the shooting would be the other way around. Mr. Rochat sometimes had an angry temper. I thought something very terrible must have happened to cause Mr. Jeanneret to shoot Mr. Rochat."

"Thank you, Mr. Jones. Your Honour, that is the completion of my cross-examination of this witness. I do not expect to re-examine him

153

at a later point in the trial." Mr. Angus resumed his seat, and the judge dismissed the witness.

Mr. Renard announced that the last witness for the prosecution was Mr. Hanna. The bailiff, waiting in the hall, led him to the witness stand. The court clerk requested that Mr. Hanna place his hand on the Bible and asked, "Do you swear to tell the truth and nothing but the truth, so help you God?"

Mr. Hanna said, "I do."

"Please say and spell your name," said the court clerk.

Mr. Hanna did so, and the questioning began. Mr. Hanna testified that he had been informed by Mr. Filipek of the shooting when he rode past the Hanna property on his way to Howser to contact the provincial police. Mr. Hanna had immediately ridden to the Rochat home and assisted Mr. Jones in caring for Mrs. Rochat, who was extremely distraught. He and Mr. Jones covered the body, taking care not to disturb any possible evidence.

When asked his reaction to the shooting by Mr. Jeanneret, he said he was greatly surprised as Mr. Jeanneret had always seemed submissive and had not shown violence. Mr. Hanna explained that most of his business dealings had been with Mr. Rochat and that he trusted his decisions and word. They had known each other since 1910, when Mr. Rochat and Mr. Jeanneret had arrived in Argenta.

As Wilbert listened to the testimony, he remembered those first dealings with Mr. Hanna, usually negotiated by Thomas. He always felt somewhat taken advantage by Thomas, and he wasn't sure if he had been given all the information about the arrangements by Thomas. However, he also remembered that Hanna had helped them out many times, including with the fires, and that he was always willing to supply equipment and wagons.

THE DISTANCE

Mr. Angus chose not to cross-examine Mr. Hanna. Judge Stanley asked Mr. Renard if he had any further witnesses. "No, sir. The prosecution rests its case."

"Very well," said Judge Stanley. "We will resume court tomorrow morning at 9:30. Mr. Angus, will you be ready to proceed with the case for the defence?"

"Yes, Your Honour."

"Court is adjourned."

The bailiff announced, "All rise." The judge walked out of the courtroom and the spectators quickly left, eager to seek out the sunlight outside. Wilbert was briskly cuffed and assisted from the room by the jail guards.

In the dreary cell, Wilbert sat slouched on the edge of the bed, waiting for his lawyer. All the evidence was against him. *Is Mr. Angus coming?* The jangle of the key in the lock startled him as he looked up to see Mr. Angus's determined face. "Wilbert, I know it sounded bad. Remember that several witnesses described you as being kind, respectable, and community minded. Tomorrow will be a different day."

"Will tomorrow ever get here? It seems like an eternity away," Wilbert mumbled. "And all I can do is sit in this miserable place."

"They'll bring food soon. Try to get some sleep. I'll come in the morning before court resumes." Mr. Angus banged on the cell door to get the attention of the guard and disappeared, leaving Wilbert to his dejection.

Gertrude and Liza remained in their seats until everybody else had left the courtroom. Liza clung to Gertrude's arm and buried her face in the soft shoulder. She whispered, "Are they gone yet? I'm afraid to stand up."

155

JUDY POLLARD

Gertrude assured her that the room was empty, slowly lifted Liza to her feet, and then led the way out of the building. Together they shuffled along the street to the hotel, avoiding any eyes that might look their way. In the room, Liza threw herself on the bed and sobbed, feeling as if her own heart was splitting open from hearing the story.

Gertrude maintained her calmness and suggested they rest for a while before finding some food. The two women laid on their beds, reliving the voices of the attorneys and witnesses, the sharpness of the judge, and the sounds of the crowd reacting to what they heard. They recalled with each other some of the damming comments that increased the fear of what would happen in the courtroom the next day. Eventually each of them was able to find a few minutes of sleep, and in the morning, Gertrude insisted they eat breakfast before setting off early to find a seat in the courthouse.

The Case for the Defence

~

Wilbert spent a long night flopping restlessly on the slab of a mattress. Sharp pangs jabbed him, penetrating his chest at the thought of a death penalty. As usual, he was relieved to leave his cell and be led back to the brightness and warmth of the courtroom. The first thing he looked for when he entered was a glimpse of Liza and Gertrude. They were sitting in the front again, and he sighed with relief. Liza's periwinkle-coloured eyes, although tired-looking, returned his gaze with affection. She was beautiful in her blue dress with the tiny white flowers, so like the Edelweiss at home in Switzerland. Even after bearing three children, her young body had vitality and strength. His devotion to her made all of this necessary.

Again, he heard the "All rise," and the judge swept into the room, robe trailing in his wake. Everyone was in their place. Wilbert shook off his thoughts of Liza and concentrated on the proceedings with a combination of apprehension and anticipation. This was the day that the defence must find a way to convince the jury that Wilbert had no other choice but to shoot Thomas and that his reasons were valid. He knew that Mr. Angus planned to call Mr. Filipek to testify.

The Filipeks were one of the closer neighbours, and Wilbert and Mr. Filipek had become friends while assisting each other with water lines

157

from Argenta Creek. Originally from the Ukraine, the Filipeks were learning English, and Wilbert often helped them to read information and write in English. Mr. Angus's decision to call Mr. Filipek as the first witness was a good one from Wilbert's perspective. He also knew that the only other witness for the defence was himself. Talking was not his favourite thing to do. Especially right now.

Judge Stanley said, "Mr. Angus, please call your first witness."

"Yes, Your Honour," said Mr. Angus. "I call Mr. Filipek to the witness stand."

The bailiff entered the courtroom leading Mr. Filipek and directed him to the witness box. The court clerk proceeded to swear in the witness and have him say and spell his name for the record.

Mr. Filipek was a short, lean man. He wore a grey, long-sleeved shirt and dark-coloured pants with suspenders, and he carried his cap in his trembling hands as he entered the witness stand. His dark hair was cut short, and he was deeply tanned. Heavy eyebrows framed his serious black eyes. He looked like he was gritting his teeth, praying this would soon be over.

Mr. Angus began, "Mr. Filipek, please explain how long you have lived in Argenta and your occupation."

In a weak voice, Mr. Filipek spoke, "In 1917, I moved to Argenta from Alberta wid my wife and family. We have land pre-emption. Want to start fruit farm."

"Please explain your relationship with Mr. Jeanneret."

"Our properties are close together and have water lines from Argenta Creek. We help each other. My wife and me, we are still learning English. Mr. Jeanneret help us because he is good in speaking and writing. He knows French also. They are good neighbours."

"Did you know Mr. Rochat?"

158

THE DISTANCE

"Yes, sir. Small place, we all help each other. Mr. Rochat was very strong. When there was a big job, we ask his help. He always helped."

"What did you know about the relationship between Mr. Rochat and Mr. Jeanneret?"

"They both came from Europe, like us. Had land pre-emption. Business partners. They were clearing the land and making orchards for about ten years, I think."

"From your perspective how did they get along with each other?"

"All right, I think. Mr. Rochat was big and talked a lot. Mr. Jeanneret is quiet and small but always worked hard. Together they did land clearing."

"Have you any knowledge of them conflicting with each other to the point of violence?"

"No, sir. I heard them arguing once or twice, like when we were building the school.

"Do you have any knowledge of Mr. Jeanneret being violent with other people or of him threatening anybody?"

"No, sir. Mr. Jeanneret is not a violent person. I think he hates violence."

"Thank you, Mr. Filipek. Your Honour, that is all I intend to ask of Mr. Filipek at this time."

Judge Stanley said, "Mr. Renard, do you wish to cross-examine this witness?"

Mr. Renard stood and stated that he intended to do so. Mr. Renard said, "Mr. Filipek, do you know if Mr. Jeanneret uses his rifle to hunt game?"

"Yes, sir. He does."

"Have you ever hunted with him?"

"Yes, sir. One time were hunting for elk. We saw a mother elk protecting her young."

"What happened?"

159

JUDY POLLARD

"Mr. Jeanneret shot the mother elk and the young one. We skinned the animals for butchering. Lots of good meat for next few months."

Mr. Renard levelled his most piercing look at Mr. Filipek and said, "You are saying that he cold-heartedly killed the mother protecting her young one? Is that how a responsible hunter should behave?"

"Depends how bad the meat needed for food. The calf wouldn't live without the mother," replied Mr. Filipek with a puzzled expression.

"Thank you, Mr. Filipek. Your Honour, that is the end of my cross-examination of this witness."

Mr. Filipek's comments about killing the elk brought back sharp memories for Wilbert. He was aware of the density of the brush with the damp smell of rain and the sound of careful steps of the elk as she tended her calf. He remembered his remorse with the decision to kill the calf. This was something he never would have considered doing before he began living in a remote place and learning that sometimes actions were taken when it seemed like the best alternative.

Judge Stanley thanked the witness, and the bailiff took him from the witness stand. The judge instructed Mr. Angus to call his next witness.

"Thank you, Your Honour," said Mr. Angus. "I call Mr. Vadas to the witness stand." Wilbert was surprised when Mr. Vadas was called as he thought Mr. Filipek was the only other witness for the defence.

The bailiff entered the courtroom leading Mr. Vadas and directed him to the witness box. The court clerk proceeded to swear in the witness and have him say and spell his name for the record.

"Mr. Vadas, please explain how long you have lived in Argenta and your occupation," said Mr. Angus.

"I have lived in Argenta for seven years. I have a small farm. I am a logger."

"What is your association with Mr. Jeanneret?"

160

THE DISTANCE

"My property is immediately north of the property where he has his house. We often meet each other on the wagon road and help haul materials to and from the wharf."

"Do your families know each other?"

"Yes, sir. Our wives are friends. Liza and Sylvie meet at the wharf on mail day and walk up the hill together. We don't have any children, but Sylvie sometimes helps Liza by looking after her children. And Liza shares her delicious cheese with us."

"How would you describe Mr. Jeanneret?"

"Serious and hardworking, quiet. Never known him to get in trouble. He doesn't say a lot. He's a family man. Doesn't drink much as far as I know."

"How would you describe his relationship with his work partner, Mr. Rochat?"

"Not sure. They've been partners a long time."

"What did you think when you heard about the shooting?"

"I couldn't believe it! There's got to be a good reason for Wilbert to go after Thomas. My wife told me that Thomas tries to give Liza a ride home in his wagon. Seems like Thomas was pretty friendly with her. I never really trusted him. Too slick and easy with women."

"What do you mean?"

"I don't like to say, but if Thomas got near my wife, I'd go after him," Mr. Vadas reddened and choked on his words. "A man has to look after his wife and his family. Who else is going to do it?"

Mumblings could be heard in the crowd of spectators. A deep voice said loudly, "You got that right!" Other voices could be heard, "I agree." "Me too." Judge Stanley banged his gavel and sternly admonished the spectators to keep silent.

161

"Do you think that was what Mr. Jeanneret was doing?" questioned Mr. Angus.

Mr. Renard jumped to his feet. "Objection, Your Honour! The defence is leading the witness." The mumblings of the people in the room became a rumble. The jury members moved restlessly in their seats.

Another voice could be heard from the back of the room, "Who wouldn't take the situation in his own hands?"

Wilbert's ears perked up when he heard the comments. *If people in the crowd understood that I had to protect my wife, what were the jury members thinking?*

Judge Stanley banged his gavel and roared, "Order in the court. I will have none of this commotion." His sharp eyes flashed at Mr. Angus. "Mr. Angus, you are leading the witness. You will not do that again."

Mr. Angus said, "Yes, Your Honour. I have no more questions for this witness."

The judge instructed the Crown attorney, Mr. Renard, to begin cross-examination if he so wished. Mr. Renard stood in front of the witness box, glowering at Mr. Vadas. With pursed lips, he said, "Mr. Vadas have you personally witnessed Mr. Rochat with Mrs. Jeanneret?"

"No sir."

"So, your comments about Mr. Rochat being too friendly with Mrs. Jeanneret are based solely on what your wife told you?"

"Yes, sir."

"Your Honour, I propose that the comments of Mr. Vadas were based on hearsay only and that they be stricken from the record," Mr. Renard announced to the judge. Mumblings could again be heard in the crowd. The judge nodded in agreement and instructed that the comments be stricken.

THE DISTANCE

Mr. Renard asked, "Have you any knowledge of Mr. Jeanneret threatening anybody in the past?"

"No, sir. I only know of him being a good neighbour."

"Thank you. Your Honour, that is the end of my cross-examination," said Mr. Renard as he sat heavily in his chair, scowling and looking annoyed. Mr. Vadas left the room hurriedly after being dismissed; his relief was evident for all to see.

Judge Stanley banged his gavel and announced a break. The bailiff instructed people to rise while the judge left the room and stated they would be called back after the lunch break.

*

WHEN THE PROCEEDINGS RESUMED AFTER lunch, Mr. Angus addressed the judge. "Your Honour, the next witness I call is Mr. Jeanneret to speak in his own defence," said Mr. Angus.

Wilbert had been engrossed in listening to Mr. Vadas and the comments that he heard from the crowd behind him. He felt reassured that Mr. Vadas had said that a man had to defend his wife. *Liza never mentioned to me that Thomas tried to give her a ride in his wagon. What is Liza thinking right now?*

He set his shoulders back and forced himself to look ahead at the judge, knowing that when he got to the witness box, he would have a hard time not looking to the crowd to see Liza. The jail guard pulled him up by his arm and led him to the box. The step up was tricky with the leg chains on his ankles and the guard pushed him impatiently. Somebody in the crowd said, "Give him a chance. Did you ever have to wear those things?" The judge glowered at the crowd again, obviously warning that he would not tolerate noise and objections.

163

Wilbert stood with his arms at his sides and listened to the court clerk repeating the oath to tell the truth as he was instructed, and then saying and spelling his name. It took intense concentration to keep his face calm and his eyes forward. Even though he was tanned, his cheeks had little of their usual healthy colouring, and he took deep breaths. He knew some of the questions and prayed that he would be able to answer in a way that people would believe him and agree with him. That was his only chance to be acquitted. The alternative was unthinkable. Liza and Gertrude huddled together, clutching hands, ears straining to hear.

Mr. Angus said, "Mr. Jeanneret, please describe to the court your relationship with Mr. Rochat, including how long it has lasted and the work partnership."

Wilbert heaved his shoulders back and looked straight in the eye of the defence lawyer. He answered hesitatingly with a low tone. "We knew each other slightly when we were in school in a French-speaking part of Switzerland. As adults, we met by chance. I was an employee of Cook's Travel Agency, and he was finishing his term with the Swiss Guard. We had a common interest in exploring opportunities in Canada and obtained a land pre-emption on Kootenay Lake. In 1909, we moved to Argenta and began developing land on the slope of Mount Willet for fruit orchards."

Judge Stanley interrupted, "Mr. Jeanneret, please speak loudly and clearly so that everybody in the court is able to hear you." Wilbert looked at the judge and nodded slightly.

Mr. Angus asked, "Have you been continuously working together in Argenta since you arrived there?"

Wilbert started to look more relaxed as the questions were the ones that Mr. Angus had prepared him for. His voice became stronger. "Yes, except when I returned to Switzerland in 1914 to find a wife. After

THE DISTANCE

Liza and I were married, we returned to live in Argenta. Shortly after that, Mr. Rochat left briefly and married one of my sisters, Rose. After their marriage, they returned to live in Mr. Rochat's house on the flats in Argenta." Wilbert spoke with humility and honesty. His face regained some of its characteristic colour and his blue eyes were earnest.

"Is it accurate to say that you were business partners who worked closely together on an almost daily basis for approximately thirteen years?"

"Yes, sir."

"Please describe how well you got along with each other."

"We were a good team at first. Thomas was big and strong and knew about cutting trees and using tools and livestock. I knew how to read and write English, so I could do paperwork and correspondence. We both helped each other learn different things. After we both got married, our wives were friends, both having come from Switzerland. And, of course, they were also sisters-in-law."

"How did you get along as the years went by?"

"There was so much hard work. It never ended, and we both got tired. Thomas accused me of being lazy even when I worked more hours on the mountain every day than he did."

"Would you say there was friction between you?" asked Mr. Angus.

"Yes, some." Wilbert dropped his eyes with embarrassment.

"Did anything else happen that caused friction between you?"

"Liza told me that Thomas, er . . . Mr. Rochat started to be too forward with her during the time we lived with the Rochats when we were building a new house. Recently, after the baby was born in the spring, Thomas began to threaten Liza if she would not cooperate with his advances."

"Your wife told you this herself?"

165

"Yes, she did."

Liza listened breathlessly, trying to close her ears, praying that nobody knew who she was.

"What was your reaction?"

"I went to his house with my shotgun and told him that he had a week's notice to leave. The next day he approached my wife again, and she came to me. I knew as long as he lived, I could not properly look after my wife, although I never had any doubt she was innocent. So I waited all night then went to his house in the morning and shot him with my rifle. I have been tormented with remorse ever since on account of his wife, daughter, and relatives.

"What do you think Mr. Rochat would have done if he were in your position?"

"Rose said that he told her he was sure I was going to shoot him. This shows that he would have shot me if he were in my place, and for him, like for me, there was only one possible way to redeem one's woman's honour." Barely concealed comments of agreement could be heard whispered through the crowd.

"Mr. Jeanneret, how would you describe yourself?"

"I think I'm honest and hardworking. I do what I say I'm going to do. I look after my wife and children as best I can, and I protect them against any wrongdoing."

"Would you say you are a violent person?"

"No, sir. I am not. In Switzerland I was raised to be a pacifist, and I have never committed violence before. In this situation, it was necessary to protect my wife and redeem her honour and the honour of my family. There was no other choice but to shoot Thomas."

Mr. Angus turned to the judge. "Your Honour, that is all the questions I have for now."

THE DISTANCE

Judge Stanley turned to the Crown attorney, Mr. Renard, and instructed him to begin cross-examination. Mr. Renard stood, then slowly walked to stand in front of Wilbert in a deliberate way, as if he were contemplating how to open his attack. Wilbert stared at the sharp-edged face and tried to return the glare. Mr. Renard spoke calmly. "Mr. Jeanneret, you testified that your wife told you she was being threatened by Mr. Rochat if she didn't comply with his advances is that true?"

"Yes, sir," Wilbert muttered with a slight nod.

"You said you needed to protect your wife and your honour." Again, Wilbert mumbled an affirmative.

"Did you see anything that made you think she was in direct peril if you did not shoot Mr. Rochat immediately?"

"No, I did not see him threaten her, but my sisters told me they saw him force her to look at him and answer him. They did not like it."

"If you thought she was in direct peril, why did you not contact the police?"

Wilbert looked at the floor, and when he finally raised his head, he said, "It would take too long. They were far away. I thought Thomas would go back to my house and threaten Liza again."

"Mr. Jeanneret, you have testified that you are an honest and responsible person, and yet you decided to take the law into your own hands without even attempting to get help from the police." It was as if the room itself held its breath waiting for Wilbert's answer. Wilbert felt the eyes of Liza and Gertrude bolstering him, lifting his chest to bring strength into his lungs.

"I am the only one who can fully protect my wife and family. I believe that Thomas would have continued to force himself on my wife. I know that there was only one way to fulfill my responsibilities to my wife and family, and that was to kill him. If I had not, he would have killed me."

167

JUDY POLLARD

The collective emphatic sigh of the courtroom very nearly shuffled the papers on the desk of the Crown prosecutor. Now all ears waited for his response.

"Your Honour, I have finished cross-examination of Mr. Jeanneret," he said with a tone of annoyance. He had also heard the response from the crowd.

Judge Stanley looked at Mr. Renard with surprise, then said, "Very well. Mr. Jeanneret, you may leave the witness stand."

The jail guard accompanied Wilbert back to the prisoner box, and Wilbert dropped onto the seat looking exhausted. Judge Stanley announced a break in the proceedings and informed the lawyers that when the court resumed, they were to give their concluding remarks.

The bailiff called, "All rise." The judge then rose and left the bench, with a look of consternation on his face. The bailiff announced the break and cleared the court.

168

The Final Summaries of the Lawyers

~

Two hours later, the court proceedings resumed. The bailiff announced, "All rise," and Judge Stanley strode to the bench. He peered with annoyance at the lawyers, the accused, and everybody in the pews. It was clear that he intended to keep a tight rein on order in the room.

"Mr. Renard, please present your summary to the court," said the judge.

"Your Honour and members of the jury, the court has been presented with clear evidence that on August 31, Mr. Jeanneret went with his rifle to the home of Mr. Rochat with the intent to shoot him. Constable Oland reported that Mr. Jeanneret waited in a shed for Mr. Rochat to leave his house in the morning and that when Mr. Rochat was nearby, he shot him in the chest. After Mr. Rochat ran a distance and then collapsed on the ground, Mr. Jeanneret walked to him and shot him in the back three times. This evidence makes it clear that Mr. Jeanneret planned the murder and carried it out with intention. He obviously showed no mercy to Mr. Rochat, his long-time business partner and brother-in-law. Mr. Jeanneret stated that although he knew Mr. Rochat had threatened his wife, he did not consider contacting the police in Kaslo for help. Furthermore, it is obvious that Mr. Jeanneret believed

169

it was necessary for him to kill Mr. Rochat, so he consciously took the matter into his own hands and did not engage assistance. Mr. Jeanneret openly stated that he shot Mr. Rochat and is clearly guilty of murder." Mr. Renard stared pointedly at each jury member in turn. Some of them returned his look; others did not, moving restlessly in their seats. Mr. Renard returned to his seat.

The crowd watched every detail, eager to hear what the defence lawyer would say in summary. Wilbert leaned forward over the table. *Everything the lawyer said was true. What could the jury possibly think but that I am guilty?* Judge Stanley thanked Mr. Renard and told Mr. Angus to begin his summary.

"Your Honour and the jury," began Mr. Angus, standing at his table, white-knuckled hands pressed onto the array of papers before him. "You see before you an honourable man. A gentle and humble man; a man who placed the highest value on the safety and well-being of his wife and family. Mr. Jeanneret has, by the accounts provided by witnesses, been known for his honesty and responsible behaviour. He has a long-standing, positive reputation in the community as an astute business-man. He has demonstrated his belief in the importance of education for children through his involvement in creating and funding a school in his community and in his continued collaboration with the schoolteacher to maintain a viable situation. All of this occurred even before his own children were old enough for full-time attendance. For the thirteen years that Mr. Jeanneret has lived in Argenta, he has consistently been a hard-working member of the community and a neighbour always ready to cooperate and assist others. All his life he has been opposed to conflict and violence and has been known as a law-abiding and peaceful person. This is the nature of Mr. Jeanneret.

THE DISTANCE

"You have heard testimony that Mr. Jeanneret became so concerned about the safety and well-being of his wife and family that he decided the only way he could ensure their continued protection was first to confront Mr. Rochat and insist that he leave the community, and then, with more evidence of threats toward Mrs. Jeanneret, to shoot Mr. Rochat. Mr. Jeanneret has stated that he was greatly pained by the decision and the knowledge of how negative the effect was on his sister, Mrs. Rochat, and other family members, yet he saw no other path. Constable Oland testified that Mr. Jeanneret was totally cooperative and compliant when he was taken into custody, and he has continued to be so throughout his incarceration in jail awaiting trial. I put it to each of you to think about how you interpret the character of Mr. Jeanneret and how it is unlikely that he would ever again make a decision to use violence to solve a problem. That is the completion of my summation. Thank you for what I know will be careful consideration of the character of Mr. Jeanneret and his significance to all his family." Mr. Angus spoke earnestly and deliberately caught the eye of each individual jury member before returning to his seat.

Judge Stanley slowly surveyed the room as if he were trying to sense the emotional tone. The observers had been attentive and respectful as the two lawyers presented summations; however, he knew that some people supported Mr. Jeanneret, and they might try to let their opinions be known in order to influence the jurors.

Finally, the Judge spoke, "Members of the jury, you have heard the evidence in the case of *Regina versus Mr. Jeanneret*, who was accused of the murder of Mr. Rochat on August 31. Mr. Jeanneret, when asked how he pleaded, remained silent, or in the interpretation of the court pleaded not guilty. The evidence of the prosecution and of the defence has been presented in detail. The weapon used to shoot Mr. Rochat has

171

been identified and entered into the court record. Mr. Jeanneret has himself stated that he shot Mr. Rochat.

"At this point, I present you with the task of determining whether Mr. Jeanneret is guilty of the charge of murder. It is imperative that you carefully consider all the evidence in an objective manner and in consideration of the law of the land. The sentence for murder is very serious and includes the death penalty; however, it is possible to add a recommendation for mercy. The court will adjourn now and resume tomorrow morning in order for you to deliver a verdict." The judge banged his gavel, and as the bailiff announced, "All rise," the judge stood and, with a flourish of his robes, moved swiftly out the door.

The bailiff cleared the courtroom, and the guards took Wilbert to his cell. As the crowd slowly exited, comments could be heard. "He's guilty, no question." "He had to do it. What else could he do?" "Glad I'm not on that jury." They would be back early the next day to find out the results. Liza and Gertrude huddled in the corner of the long seat, again wanting to be the last to leave.

Gertrude, trying to be understanding, said, "Liza, we have to leave. The bailiff is coming toward us."

"Did you hear what they were saying?" Liza whispered as she vibrated with dread.

Gertrude's strong hands helped her to stand, and then with an arm around her waist, she led her out the door. "We will eat and then I'll make sure that Wilbert's clean shirt is delivered to his cell for the morning. He needs to at least look clean, and it might help him feel better."

Wilbert felt glued to his seat. The jail guard tugged at his arm and forced him to stand and shuffle yet again in the leg chains. He barely noticed over the racket in his brain. His stomach twisted at the thought of this night in the cell. He knew there would be no rest.

The Verdict

~

It was morning at last. Wilbert paced around his cell, his head thumping. He'd had no sleep and had no appetite for the paltry breakfast. He dressed in his slacks and tweed jacket for the final day he was going to court. He appreciated that Gertrude had sent him a clean shirt so he had something fresh to wear. The jail guards appeared, cuffed him, and led him on the slow walk to the courtroom. They stopped in the hallway outside the entrance to the room. On the other side of the door, they heard the hubbub of people chattering and pushing to be the first to get seats. Those that had been coming every day thought they were entitled to be first. Loud demands were heard: "Hey that's my seat!" "I've had that seat every day!"

The bailiff made his announcement that people would not be allowed to stand and must leave. Finally, after the crowd settled into place, he opened the side door, and the guards led Wilbert to the prisoner box. Wilbert dragged himself along. He needed to see Liza and Gertrude, and he halted and looked to the front bench. There they were, both waiting for him. He took a breath and stepped into the box and sat. *Can I make himself listen to what will be said today?*

Members of the jury filed in and took their seats. The bailiff called out, "All rise. The court is in session." Judge Stanley breezed through the

173

door, his black cloud billowing behind him and sat in his prestigious chair. All sat down, and the room held its breath.

Judge Stanley addressed the jury, "Gentlemen of the jury, have you decided on a verdict?"

The jury foreman stood and responded in a shaky voice, "Yes, Your Honour, we have."

"What is your verdict?"

"Your Honour, we find the accused, Mr. Jeanneret, not guilty of the murder, by a unanimous vote to acquit him."

Judge Stanley appeared taken aback by the statement. He glared from person to person in the jury box as if he didn't believe the statement that they could all agree on the verdict. Each person kept eyes down as if refusing to be influenced. The foreman sat timidly in his seat as the judge collected his thoughts.

The judge trembled with anger when he finally spoke. "The evidence presented in this trial is indisputable that there was a threat to kill, followed by the killing itself after the lapse of several hours, during which the accused and the deceased were not near each other, although the deceased had been given a week to leave the country. Undaunted by these facts, the accused pleaded self-defence, which must seem a mockery to anyone who heard him. To speak plainly, the only verdict open on the evidence was that of murder, and if the jury saw fit, they could have added a recommendation to mercy.

"But because the jury has unanimously agreed that Mr. Jeanneret is not guilty, I must pronounce the verdict as such and acquit Mr. Jeanneret. The result of this verdict is that a self-confessed murderer is allowed to go scot-free by a jury of his peers, and for the first time, as far as I know, a special kind of lynch law has been sanctioned in this country,

THE DISTANCE

as it makes no difference in principle whether the victim is slain by one man who lurks in ambush or by a mob who openly attacks him."

The room exploded with colliding opinions: "He had to do it!" "He murdered and should pay a price!"

Liza and Gertrude, feeling the tumult behind them, shrunk in their seats, mouths agape with astonishment. Wilbert buried his head in his hands and tried to stop the racket. He searched for his thoughts in the maelstrom. During the night, he had started thinking about what might happen if he wasn't convicted and realized that if he went back to Argenta he would need his rifle.

Wilbert, suddenly emboldened by the disturbance behind him, jumped to his feet. "Your Honour. May I speak please?" Judge Stanley gaze shot spears into Wilbert's eyes as he nodded yes.

"I want to apply for an order to have my shotgun and rifle returned to me. I have need of both to sustain my livelihood in Argenta, in order to provide meat for my table and protection if necessary for my family."

People in the crowd quieted again, as if astonished that Wilbert would have the presence of mind to make such application. Judge Stanley sternly responded, "I refuse the application inasmuch as a verdict of murder was the only verdict open on the evidence; the administration of the law should not be further discredited by the return of the weapons to the assassin." His voice rose with the force of his anger, and he said as he pounded his mallet, "I reject the application! Court is adjourned!" The judge rushed from the room before the bailiff had a chance to call, "All rise."

People milled and pushed around, several of them shouting congratulations to Wilbert. The reporter from the *Nelson Daily News* elbowed his way through the crowd and tried to get the attention of Wilbert. Mr. Angus, with his back to the reporter, was at Wilbert's side, blocking

175

JUDY POLLARD

access. Liza and Gertrude managed to squeeze between people and wrapped their arms around Wilbert. All three stood trying to talk and yet were so shocked that the words were hard to find. Wilbert asked Mr. Angus, "What happens now?"

Mr. Angus explained that he was free. He was allowed to collect any possessions from the jail cell and to leave the court with Liza and Gertrude. The jail guard removed the leg irons and brought Wilbert's few possessions from the cell while the three spoke together. Wilbert, Liza, and Gertrude were all hesitant to leave the court and go outside until the crowd diminished. They weren't ready to face curious people and reporters. Mr. Angus encouraged them to go to the hotel where Liza and Gertrude had been staying and then plan how they would return to Argenta. He said that he would visit them that evening to explain how the verdict would be recorded and reported to Wilbert and to present an invoice for his services.

When Mr. Angus arrived that evening, the three of them were sitting at the dining table waiting. Wilbert asked, "What did you find out?"

"The court judgment will be mailed to you within a month," said Mr. Angus, "and it is clear that the prosecution will not be appealing the verdict, in case you were worried about that."

"That is a relief, although I hadn't really thought about it. Thank you for all your help. I will need to correspond with my bank and send you what I owe for your services," explained Wilbert. "It might take a few days."

Gertrude, speaking on behalf of all three, interrupted. "All we want to do now is go back home to Argenta. Did you find out if the *Moyie* has a trip scheduled tomorrow?"

176

THE DISTANCE

"I understand. And yes, the *Moyie* sails tomorrow morning at seven o'clock. I'm sure you're exhausted so I'll leave now and wish you a good night."

Each of them thanked him again for his services and shook his hand warmly before he left.

*

"As I think about the situation, I'm almost aghast at the simplicity of the outcome after the long and complex story. The fortunes of the Jeannerets had completely turned around. It's difficult to imagine what might have been going through their minds, and regardless of the turmoil, they needed to take the next steps and get back home."

Hans responded, "They had so much to cope with. It must have been confusing and exhausting!"

The Journey and Home

~

The early morning walk to the *Moyie* dock was only a few minutes long; however, Wilbert's eyes struggled with the bright fall sunlight after the confinement of jail. Each carried a small case with only a few belongings. They hurried, eager to be the first in line to get passenger tickets. Wilbert paused as he noticed a slender man, dressed in slacks, a blazer, and a grey fedora hat, striding purposefully toward him. The man wore spectacles and had alert grey eyes. He offered a handshake and said, "How do you do? I'm Harry McArthur. I was fascinated by the trial and keen to meet you."

Wilbert responded to the handshake with surprise. "How do you do, sir? Are you from a newspaper?"

Harry chuckled. "No, I'm a teacher in Nelson, about to assume the principalship of a new school, and a strong advocate of education. Your obvious dedication to creating a school in your community is admirable. Congratulations on the not guilty verdict. I'm sure you're exhausted and eager to board the boat for your trip home."

"Yes, that is true indeed. It is very nice to meet you. Now we must continue to the boat to purchase our tickets," said Wilbert with a slight nod. "Good-bye." He glanced at Liza and Gertrude and led them to the line-up that was beginning to form at the ticket office. Liza, looking over

179

JUDY POLLARD

her shoulder, smiled at Harry, appreciative that he had been comple-
mentary to Wilbert, especially under the circumstances.

The purser found a cabin with bunk beds that they could rent rather
than sit in the lounge with the group of passengers. Gertrude offered
cash for the extra fare, and the three entered the room that had two
small cots and two chairs as well as a miniature wash basin.

"Thank you, Gertrude. I didn't know how I could sit with all the other
people," whispered Liza. "Some of them might have been at the trial."

Each of them was exhausted in their own way. They had little sleep
the night before, their brains tumbling after the previous days in court,
and not really believing that it was over. They could go home. They
sat motionless, squeezed together on the edge of the small bunk bed,
waiting for the sound of the ship engine, the splash of the paddles, and
the blast of the horn that would signal the beginning of the long boat
ride to the north end of Kootenay Lake. It was as if they had forgotten
how to talk to each other.

"I'm going to find breakfast," announced Gertrude, and she left the
room for Liza and Wilbert.

Wilbert slouched in the corner of the bed, his body drained of
strength. Liza watched and wondered if she should talk. "I just want to
go home and see my children," she said softly.

Wilbert nodded. "Me too." He searched her eyes for the usual brightness, dismayed that he couldn't find her spirit. His face wrinkled with a
mixture of confusion and relief. "When we get home, we can finally get
some rest."

"Well, remember the children, and the cow, and the garden, and, and,
and . . ." Liza smiled. "Maybe right now you can get some sleep on the
cot. I want to try to lie down. We have time for a rest before we dock
in Argenta."

180

THE DISTANCE

Seven hours later, the *Moyie* finally docked in Argenta, and although several people were on the wharf, there was nobody to greet them. All three of them were relieved because they couldn't face talking with their neighbours after all they'd been through. They knew that Millie would be at the house with the children and preparing dinner. They hadn't sent notice of when they would arrive, so it would be a surprise for everyone.

Gertrude, always practical, suggested that she go on ahead to let Millie know that they were on their way. "You take as much time as you want to get to the house. It'll be overwhelming to suddenly be back."

Liza nodded and said, "Thanks, that's appreciated."

Liza and Wilbert walked slowly up the wagon road, around the curves and ditches, smelling the rich underbrush that had just begun drying out in the fall. A soft breeze rustled the high branches on the pine and cedar trees. Wilbert heard the high-pitched repetitive screech of an osprey, floating high overhead, easily identified by the characteristic inverted 'V' on the underside of its wings. Oxygen filled the air and permeated their lungs. At last, they were beginning to breathe again. Wilbert commented, "The air in the courthouse was dead, and it made me feel dead."

Liza nodded in agreement, tears sneaking down her cheeks. The hurt was too fresh to talk about. As they made their way to their gate, she said, "Everything looks the same. Like nothing has happened. So hard to believe. I don't know how to think."

"I didn't know if I would ever see our perfect Swiss house again. And there it is, a mirage in the distance. Do I deserve another chance?" asked Wilbert.

"For the sake of our children, I want us to recreate our home and find a way to put the ugliness behind us. And Wilbert, look behind the

181

house. There's the guardian mountain supporting us as it always has," Liza said with determination.

The aromas of hash browns and onions and rich cheese greeted them as they walked up the final stretch of the path, past the flourishing vegetable garden and onto the porch. The door was flung open by Jessie, shrieking and throwing herself at Liza. "Mama, Mama, you're home! We have supper. I helped Millie make rosti. And Pete and I found morel mushrooms too!" Millie rushed to Daniel to keep him from throwing himself out of his chair to join his brother and sister.

Pete launched himself at Wilbert, demanding a ride on his back. "Papa, I've been waiting for you!"

Hugs, tears, and laughter echoed throughout the house. Daniel demanded a perch on Liza's lap and snuggled against her. Pete and Jessie mobbed Wilbert, leaping and shouting, "You're home, you're home!"

Millie spoke, astonished, "What happened? You are home, Wilbert!! You are all home. What does this mean?"

Gertrude asked if there was enough food for them and when Millie nodded, she suggested they all sit down and eat together. Bellies were soon filled with potato-rich rosti. The telling of the trial story would wait until after the children were settled in their beds for the night.

Late Summer 1932

~

"That must be the Johnson's Landing wharf that we're pulling into now," I commented to Hans. "I hope you found the story compelling."

Hans, with a friendly grin, nodded his enthusiastic interest. "Thank you for telling me and enlivening the long boat trip. I hope you find the family you are looking for so you can complete the story after these ten years that have passed since the trial."

"And goodbye to you and good fortune in your effort to make contact with your family member."

The *Moyie* was soon under steam again, travelling the last few miles north to the Argenta wharf. It was to be docked longer than usual because of a large shipment of fruit to go out that had to be handled carefully. The purser mentioned that the unloading and reloading will likely take about three hours. I hoped that was enough time to hike up the mountain path and go to the Jeanneret house for a short visit.

"Excuse me," I said to the young teenager standing on the dock. "Can you direct me to the Jeanneret house?"

"Why do you want to go there?" he asked.

JUDY POLLARD

"I met Mr. Jeanneret briefly about ten years ago, and I've always wanted to come to Argenta and see where he and the family live. He probably won't remember me."

"He remembers everything! You might be surprised even if it was so long ago."

"That would be good."

"I can take you there," he replied. "I'm Pete Jeanneret. I'm getting the mail and then going home, so you can come with me."

I noticed his dark hair, sharp blue eyes, and rosy cheeks. He reminded me of the way Wilbert looked when I saw him the day after the trial: a robust and healthy-looking lad. He pointed to the path leading up the mountain and strode ahead of me, setting a challenging pace.

"How far is it to the farm?"

"About a mile. Usually takes me half an hour to get to the house."

Eventually we passed through a large, fenced garden and were on the doorstep of the house. A slightly stooped, almost bald man walked toward us from the barn door and called out, "Pete, who have you got there?"

I quickly offered my hand. "Mr. Jeanneret, I'm Harry McArthur. Your son kindly offered to show me the way to your farm, as I don't know my way around Argenta."

"Hmm, nice to meet you," answered Wilbert Jeanneret, as his suspicious eyes carefully scanned my appearance. "Have we met before?"

"Yes, Mr. Jeanneret, ten years ago in Nelson. I introduced myself to you when you were on your way home after the trial. I attended all the proceedings and was fascinated by the outcome. I'm a school teacher and told you that I was impressed with the testimonies that you had been instrumental in starting the school in Argenta and that you personally had donated considerable funds."

184

THE DISTANCE

"I do remember you now. I don't know if I thanked you for your comments at the time. I was exhausted and wanted to get on the boat and get home," Wilbert said with a small smile. "What brings you here today?"

"I have a new position and am moving to Kamloops soon. I have thought about you many times and wanted to find out what happened after the trial before I left the Kootenays, so I came on the *Moyie* today."

"Come in and have a cup of tea, and you can meet my wife, Liza," said Wilbert.

"I would appreciate that. Thank you so much. I have only two hours and then I have to be back at the *Moyie*. Tea would refresh me after the hike up the mountain."

The home was warm and friendly, designed and decorated in a Swiss style, with lace curtains and crocheted table coverings. The other three children came to meet me, all with the rosy cheeks and good health of their father. Liza offered a delicious cake to all of us, then shooed the children out to do garden chores. Wilbert and Liza explained that the ten years had been filled with hard work and a busy family life, including the birth of another daughter. Several years ago, Liza had taken the two daughters home to Switzerland to meet the families there, and a sister had returned with them to stay in Argenta.

I left the home with a feeling of satisfaction in knowing that Wilbert and Liza had pulled their lives together and moved forward in supporting their children. They were very involved with the school and an asset to the community. My mind was mystified as I realized that in the two-hour conversation there was not one mention of the murder and trial and how those events effected and shaped either of them and their relationship. I thought of the many questions remaining from the trial itself: the legal issues; the changes in the rights of women in society; the views towards men and their property rights, including rights over their wives.

As the *Moyie* pulled away from the wharf, I gazed at the massive bulk of the watchful guardian, Mount Willet. It was as if the ever-knowing presence that allowed for the acceptance of the truths of life and death had somehow contributed to the remarkable outcome of the story.

The trip back to Nelson gave me much time to ponder and to be grateful that I was returning to my own family and my strong sons. I knew that this was a story that would stay with me for the rest of my life, and maybe I would share with my grandchildren someday. I drew my journal from my pack and began to pour out my thoughts and questions. I found it hard to believe that after the exhaustion of the murder and trial it would be possible for Wilbert and Liza to resume their previous life and relationship so smoothly and closet their thoughts and feelings from themselves and their world. A fourth child was born three years after they returned to their farm. How did they return to marital relations after all that happened? Today they had seemed to display the image of a strong couple and a strong family.

What might be Liza's reflections on the events, her emotional losses, and her choices about securing the future for herself and her children? As a woman, she had little power and financial stability without a husband, so might she have felt trapped and unable to do anything other than be the obedient, hard-working wife. What was her opinion of Wilbert when he became a murderer? Could she have found him threatening?

Another question that haunted me was how the members of the community responded to the Jeannerets after the trial. Perhaps they decided that in such a small community it was best to be neighbourly. I imagine some answers to these questions might have been exposed in letters written by Liza to her sisters in the years following the return of Wilbert to Argenta. Perhaps before making the trip to Switzerland with her daughters, Liza might have written such a letter.

THE DISTANCE

My visit with the family gave me reason to believe that there was a settlement within Wilbert and Liza and a determination to continue with their lives in the best ways possible.

EPILOGUE

~

February 1926

My dear sisters,

It is such a pleasure to write to you and express myself in French. Even though I have learned to be comfortable speaking English, I'm still poor at writing English. My exciting news is that I will soon be travelling to visit and bringing my two beautiful daughters. Jessie is now seven years old, and little Marie is just a year old. It will be a long journey, and I'm delighted to have Jessie's help with Marie as we travel. The two girls are so reliant on each other, it's like they don't even need their mother. And even though I speak French sometimes, this will be the first experience they have in situations where everyone is speaking French, so I hope at least Jessie will start using the language.

Four years have passed since the terrible time of Wilbert's trial. I can never thank you enough for being here with us during those days. As I look back now, I realize how numbed I was by everything that happened and how terrified I was at the prospect of losing my husband and being a widow. I can only be grateful that did not happen. Wilbert has always been a kind and gentle husband and a good provider for all of us, and that is most important in my mind.

Now I have a great sense of relief. Our home is safe and warm, the garden is bountiful, and the children are healthy. Wilbert and I work together as a strong team. Although the cloud in the past is never talked about, that may be for the best. I believe we will always feel protected by our mountain.

I was relieved when I received your letter telling of Rose's new situation. From what she wrote to you, it seems that she is pleased with her new husband and his family and enjoying living in a different community. I have had no contact with her but often wondered how she is. Perhaps she feels better off now that years have passed and she has a fresh start in her life.

At first it was awkward to talk and work with our neighbours; however, they seemed most interested in getting on with their lives and being part of a community in which we all need each other, so it's no longer an issue. Wilbert's strong leadership in our small community school, along with his financial donations, have made a positive impression. Nobody has ever commented or questioned Wilbert or me about the trial. Obviously some neighbours were involved at the time, so perhaps

THE DISTANCE

they discreetly told others what happened, and that was enough to satisfy their curiosity.

When we arrive in June, it will be delightful to share hugs and kisses and laughs. Jessie is especially excited. She talks about the trip every day. I'm enclosing a picture of our house that she has drawn for you.

I will write next month with more specific travel dates.

Au revoir, je t'amour,

Liza

Printed in Canada